To all the "hyper kids" out there:

You can be heroes too!

HyperKid v BullBorg

THE ADVENTURES OF HYPERKID

BOOK 1

HYPERKID v BULLBORG

BY EMERSON DAUB AND RICHARD DAUB

Published by Clay Road Press.

Written by Emerson Daub and Richard Daub.

www.hyperkid.xyz

Page layout, cover design, and images by Clay Road Press.

ISBN: 978-0-9788298-8-9

CHAPTER 1

I always knew that I was a little different than the other kids at West Plains Elementary. Mommy and Daddy say that every person in the world is different in one way or another, but you wouldn't know it because most of them don't show these differences in public so that on the outside they look just like the rest of the crowd. They also say that being different can be a very good thing. The most successful people in life are the ones who are able to embrace their differences and use them to break away from the pack. Besides, they say, it's boring trying to be like everyone else. The coolest kids in school are cool because they aren't afraid of being different, and they aren't worried about trying to hide their differences in order to fit in. If they just tried to fit in and be like everyone else, nobody would think they were cool or even notice them in the first place.

Maybe Mommy and Daddy are right, but sometimes I think they forget how hard it is to be a nine year old, especially one like me. It's really embarrassing when the teacher calls on you and you don't know the answer, or that you have to ask to repeat the question because you weren't paying attention, or that your handwriting is the sloppiest in the class, or that you're constantly being pulled from the classroom to go to group lessons that most of the other kids don't have to go to.

But the absolute worst thing in the world is when you have to stay in for recess to finish the classwork that you didn't get done earlier. This happens to me sometimes because I am easily distracted and sometimes have trouble focusing on what I am supposed to be doing. It doesn't seem fair that I get punished because of it while the other kids are outside or in the gym having fun. It makes me feel stupid when this happens. Mommy and Daddy say that I'm not stupid at all and that I'm probably one of the smartest kids in my class, but I just have to work a little harder than others at sitting still and focusing. I actually know that I'm not stupid because I know a lot of things that the other kids don't, but whenever I do have to stay in for recess I still feel stupid anyway.

That's why I wish I didn't have to go to school. And that's why I was so happy when third grade was finally over and I had the whole summer to play and have fun, which Mommy and Daddy tried to ruin by making me practice my reading and writing and math facts every day.

During the summer I also had to keep taking the medicine that I had started taking every morning and evening at the beginning of third grade to help me stay calm and focused. Without it I can get a little too wild, which Dr. Popsicle calls "hyperactive". He says it's not a big deal to be hyperactive and that lots of people, including famous movie stars and professional athletes, are hyperactive and have to take medicine to help them stay calm and focus on their jobs. While the medicine does help me stay calm, it doesn't always help with my emotions, like being too mad or too sad when something doesn't go my way, but that I will get better at controlling these feelings when I reach "the age of reason". I have no idea what that means, but Mommy and Daddy say that it's when I become more mature when I get old like when I'm eleven or twelve.

Towards the end of that summer before fourth grade, I began feeling depressed that school was going to start soon. I started having dreams that I showed up at school and had forgotten to put my pants on and all the other kids laughed at me, and another where we were playing tennis in gym class and I swung the racket and missed and the ball hit me in the nose and the other kids laughed at me again. I don't know why Mommy and Daddy think it's so great to be different, especially if it means that the other kids are always laughing at you when you have trouble doing stuff.

Then one morning a couple of weeks before school started, I suddenly realized that I was going to find out what it's like to *really* be different than the other kids.

It all started when I was brushing my teeth and noticed a cyborg who kind of looked like me staring back at me in the mirror while brushing his own teeth. I thought I was just having a really cool dream because I think cyborgs are awesome and they are in my dreams all the time. I also thought I was going to wake up at any moment, but a few minutes later when I still hadn't woken up, I began to think that maybe this wasn't a dream. Then I remembered thinking that my face did feel a little strange when I was putting on my glasses earlier. I had ignored it at the time, but when I touched my face again it felt the same way. I now realized that this wasn't a dream. *I had transformed into a real cyborg!*

My right eye was now a glowing red light, and my eye socket and a good part of my cheek, forehead, and nose was covered with a face plate made of the special grade of fortified titanium alloy compound that all leading cyborgs prefer. In my state of morning sleepiness, I hadn't noticed until now that my right forearm and hand had also been transformed into a cyborg forearm and hand. There was a little flap on the forearm that I opened, and inside there was a panel with ten different colored buttons that I was afraid to touch because I didn't know what was going to happen. The sight of the buttons brought a whole new reality to the situation, and suddenly I felt very scared.

"Mommy!" I screamed. "Mommy, come quick! I turned into a cyborg!"

Mommy was in the kitchen making breakfast, but I heard Daddy rushing up the stairs and telling me to stay calm like he always does when I get upset. Sometimes I get too upset over little things and he tells me that the problem would be solved faster if I stayed calm so that my mind could figure out what to do. But this time when he saw me, he stopped and opened his mouth like he was in shock.

"Wow!" he said when he was able to speak again. "Where did you get that cool cyborg mask? It's very realistic!"

"It's not a mask!" I exclaimed.

"What do you mean?"

He must have thought I was being silly, and when I'm being silly he usually plays along with me. But this time he suddenly became serious when he started inspecting the mask and then tried to pull it off.

"Ouch!" I said.

"Did you super glue this mask on your face?" he asked.

"It's not a mask! It's real! Look at my arm!"

At that point I started crying, which is

when he finally realized that I wasn't being silly. He called Mommy to come upstairs right away, then he hugged me and told me to stay calm and that we would figure this out. I began to think about how I always wondered what it would be like to be a real cyborg, but now that it had actually happened I wasn't so sure that I wanted to find out.

When Mommy came upstairs, she stopped and stared at me with her mouth wide open like Daddy had done earlier.

"It's not a mask," Daddy told her calmly. "Morgan has transformed into a real cyborg."

Mommy must have believed him because her eyes glazed over and then she fainted. Daddy went over to help her, but before I realized what was happening, my new red cyborg eye started scanning her body. Then a message appeared on a screen that must have been behind my eye even though it looked like it was in front of me:

POUR COLD WATER ON VICTIM

Then, without me controlling it, my new cyborg hand reached for a cup, filled it with cold water from the sink, then extended all the way to Mommy and dumped it on her face. A few seconds later Mommy started rubbing her eyes and asked Daddy what happened.

"You fainted when you saw that Morgan had turned into a cyborg," he said. She turned to look at me and promptly fainted again. At least this time she was already on the floor. My cyborg eye started scanning her again and my cyborg hand that was still holding the cup reached to the sink to refill it with water.

"Wait!" Daddy said. I thought he was going to tell me not to do it again, but instead he said he wanted a turn. He took the cup, filled it with water, and then poured it on Mommy's face.

Once again Mommy woke up, but this time Daddy told *her* to stay calm.

"Is our son really a cyborg?" she asked.

"That's right!" Daddy said excitedly.

Just then, our old cat Ralston walked in, and I couldn't believe my eyes.

"And so is the cat!" I said.

CHAPTER 2

We live in the town of West Plains, and during that same morning when I discovered I had transformed into a cyborg, we also found out that a meteor shower had hit West Plains and the neighboring town of East Plains during the night. I kind of remembered having a dream that there was a strange glowing green light outside my window that made the whole world light up. I like to sleep with the curtains open, and Ralston usually sleeps next to my feet on the bed, so Daddy thinks that the meteor shower caused the green light outside, and that the light must have been radioactive. Being exposed to this radioactive light through the window may have turned us both into cyborgs.

After recovering from her initial shock, Mommy was still very worried about me and made an appointment with Dr. Popsicle—or, "Doc Pop", as Daddy calls him.

Daddy is usually silly except when I'm doing something that I'm not supposed to be doing or when my little brother Parker is sick. Parker is five years younger than me and has asthma, so sometimes he has trouble breathing and they have to use a machine called a nebulizer that sprays his medicine through a mask that he breathes through for ten minutes or so. He doesn't seem to mind, but I'm glad I only have to take my little pills, which Mommy and Daddy break into little pieces and put in apple sauce to kill the bad taste and help me swallow them. It's too bad that we both have to take medicine, but Mommy and Daddy say that most people have at least some sort of little health problems to deal with, and that it is fortunate that what we have are treatable things we can deal with and live normal lives. Not everyone is that lucky.

Mommy wanted to set up an appointment for Ralston to see the vet as well, but Daddy didn't want to. He wanted Ralston to stay as a cyborg cat so that he could start feeding himself and clean his own litter box—and, with a little training, maybe also vacuum the floors, do the laundry, mow the lawn, and cook meals for us. Since I am the family expert on cyborgs, I informed him that while cyborg cats can do things that normal cats aren't capable of, they are not able to do any of those things he wanted Ralston to do.

"What a gyp," Daddy said disappointedly.

CHAPTER 3

Doc Pop was even sillier than Daddy. At my last checkup, he pretended that I was taking Mommy to the doctor for her checkup instead of the other way around. Usually I liked going to see Doc Pop (except when I knew that I would be getting a shot), but today was different because Mommy was worried. She didn't want anyone to notice that I was a cyborg, so she made me wear one of Daddy's hoodies and a pair of novelty eyeball glasses to cover the cyborg parts on my face. Earlier, Daddy complimented Mommy by saying she had outdone herself with the new "Unabomber" costume she had made for me. Mommy is really good at sewing and has made many Halloween costumes for me, but this time she responded by giving Daddy an annoyed look. When I asked what a "Unabomber" was, she said that he was a real life bad guy and that Daddy was only making a bad joke.

The novelty eyeball glasses had little holes cut in them so that my real eyes could see. With my new cyborg eye, I was able to scan things like cars and buildings and even people. I didn't even need my real glasses anymore because I now had super vision that could zoom in on things far away. The information from the scans appeared on a screen behind my cyborg eye that only I could see, and it would say what kind of car it was or what the address of the building or house was, and for people it just said if it was a male or a female adult or child citizen. If it was a police officer or a mail carrier or some other official person, it would say "POLICE OFFICER" or "POSTAL CARRIER" or whatever that person was.

I now also had a super hearing option that I was able to adjust by focusing on an audio level bar on the cyborg screen. The level ranged from normal to super enhanced, which I knew was a really good feature because super hearing sometimes causes problems for super heroes. When you can hear every conversation in the world, it can make you go crazy or give you a really bad headache.

My muscles felt stronger as well, and when we got out of the car I decided to test them. When Mommy wasn't looking, I lifted the car two feet off the ground and gently put it back down—which was totally awesome!

When we got to Doc Pop's office, we sat and waited for a really long time and watched the waiting kids being called in one door and the finished kids emerging from another door sucking popsicles of all different colors. Normally Mommy would comment on how silly it was that a doctor would be giving away frozen sugar all day, but today she seemed a little distracted.

When it was finally our turn, we went back to one of the examination rooms and waited another fifteen minutes or so before Doc Pop finally came in with his usual big smile. He always had a joke ready, and today he said to me, "Excuse me, sir, I am a pediatrician, which means that I only treat children, not fully grown adults like yourself."

"I am a kid!" I said and laughed.

"Why are you wearing that disguise, anyway? Did you rob a bank?"

I laughed again, but Mommy was not amused. She told me to take off my hood and glasses.

"We're here because of this," she said, pointing to my new cyborg face and holding up my new cyborg hand.

"Cool!" Doc Pop said. "Was this a birthday present? My older son would love a cyborg costume like this. It's very realistic. Did he glue it on with super glue or some industrial grade adhesive? I get cases like this more than you would think."

"No!" Mommy said loudly. "My son has really turned into a cyborg!" I felt a little scared because Mommy almost never raised her voice, even when I was having one of my meltdowns.

"Why did you turn your son into a cyborg?" Doc Pop asked.

"I didn't! We think it was the meteor shower last night because the cat turned into a cyborg too. Can you fix him?"

"The cat or your son?"

"My son!"

"Well, I'm a people doctor, not a cyborg doctor, but I've heard about cases such as this from a mechanic named Sven who owns a little shop down the block called Sven's Garage and Body Shop. He works on all sorts of stuff over there. Maybe he can take a look."

"Isn't there a medical specialist I can take him to?" Mommy asked. She looked very annoyed.

"Sven is very good," he said. "He has a bunch of specialists working for him. They work on imports, motorcycles, and even stuff like vacuum cleaners and robots. But I know he's also got some top secret stuff going on over there. He's a real character, that Sven!"

"My son is not a motorcycle or a vacuum cleaner or a robot!" Mommy said. "I need someone who can turn him back into a regular nine year old!"

"Well, then I'm afraid the only thing I can do is give you a popsicle," Doc Pop said. "I have orange, grape and cherry, but we're all out of the blue raspberry. The kids just love that blue raspberry and how it makes their tongues blue!"

CHAPTER 4

On the way home I could tell that Mommy was still upset. She kept saying that we would find a doctor who could turn me back into a normal nine year old kid, but I was already getting used to being a cyborg and liked all the cool new stuff I could now do. Back at Doc Pop's office I kept thinking that if the other kids knew I was a cyborg, they would wish they could be like me! Before today, it had always felt like I was different than the other kids, and sometimes it made me feel left out and sad. Now that I was a cyborg, I really liked being different. I didn't want to go back to being like everyone else.

"I want to stay as a cyborg!" I said to Mommy. "I don't want to change back!"

"I can't let you go back to school as a cyborg," Mommy said calmly. "I don't think cyborgs are allowed in fourth grade—or any other grades."

"But what if you can't find a doctor who can change me back?"

"I don't know. But I'm sure there's one out there. Maybe in Sweden. Or India. There seem to be a lot of medical specialists in Sweden and India."

I didn't know what Mommy was talking about and stopped listening when something started happening with my cyborg eye. A screen appeared in front of my field of vision that was some kind of high tech video grid with an image of me with my cyborg mask and arm. Then the words "GREEN METEOR TYPE" appeared, and something that looked like a laser started scanning my full body image before isolating the cyborg mask and arm. The mask and arm were then enlarged and some really fast calculations started being made. The image of my body then turned into a set of blueprints, and the cyborg parts were then covered with skin. When it was finished, I realized that these were plans for a special mask and glove that would cover my cyborg parts and make me look like my regular self. I thought this was cool until it said that the order was processing from the Shanghai SuperTech Corp in China:

A few seconds later, the images disappeared and the words "THANK YOU FOR YOUR ORDER" appeared before the screen shut down and my normal vision returned. I got nervous that I had accidentally ordered something, like the time I accidentally ordered five new refrigerators that Mommy had been looking at online that showed up in a big truck the next day. But this time it wouldn't be my fault because I didn't touch anything, so

I told Mommy what had just happened. She said not to worry about it as if she was distracted and didn't realize what I was telling her.

When we got home, though, Mommy checked her phone and saw that she had received an order confirmation message with a picture of the mask and glove. The message said that the items were being produced in China and would ship by supersonic triple express later that day, and that they would be at our house first thing in the morning. There was also a message in the notes section saying that the order was being paid for by an undisclosed third party donor.

"Well, I guess that solves that problem," Daddy said.

"No it doesn't!" Mommy said. "It just covers up the problem! The problem is that our son will still be a cyborg!"

"But I want to be a cyborg!" I said. I felt like I was about to start crying, which I do sometimes even when I get upset about things that aren't that important. But this was the most important thing ever. Even though Mommy and Daddy were always telling me how smart and special I was, I sometimes felt like the other kids were smarter and more special than me. They seemed better than me at everything from math to reading to writing to playing sports and everything else you could imagine. Sometimes I even wondered if something was wrong with me. Mommy and Daddy said there was nothing wrong with me, and that I was perfectly capable of being good at these things too if I really wanted to, but that I would just have to try a little harder to get there. I would have to stay focused and really apply myself towards achieving my goals. They would go on and on about how some of the most successful people in the world had challenges to overcome that others didn't, and because of these additional challenges, they learned how to try harder than everyone else and ultimately became more successful. Once you truly start trying to do something and putting your maximum effort into it, your fear of failure starts to disappear and your confidence begins to build. Confidence is one of the main ingredients of success. On and on and on they went about stuff like this. After a while their words started to sound the same: *blah blah blah, blah blah, blah.* I never really understood what they were trying to tell me, but now it was starting to make sense. I did feel more confident, and with this confidence I felt like I could do anything. I didn't want to lose that feeling.

"This is important!" I said. "I have super powers! I can help people!"

Mommy and Daddy looked at each other.

"I don't know," Mommy said. "Daddy and I will have to talk about it."

"If you make me a costume, I can be a real super hero!" I cried.

"What would you call yourself?" Daddy asked.

I thought about it for a moment, then it hit me like a meteor: "HyperKid!"

I thought this was the perfect name because super heroes usually name themselves after one of their main characteristics or abilities, and being hyper was certainly one of mine. I could have gone with "CyborgKid", but that sounded weird and scary. I still felt more human than cyborg, and I thought that maybe I would be able to use my natural hyper energy with my new cyborg powers to fight injustice on the playgrounds of West Plains. More than anything, though, "HyperKid" just sounded cool.

I could tell Mommy and Daddy were considering it, and I didn't want to stop the momentum.

"Maybe my new cyborg powers will even help me be less hyper at school so that I can focus on my work better," I said. "I can be regular Morgan at school with my new disguise, and then after school I can do my homework and then be HyperKid and help other kids who need it. Pleeeeeeeeeeeeeeease!"

Mommy and Daddy looked at each other again. They said they would talk about it, so they went into the other room where they thought I couldn't hear them, but they forgot that I now had super cyborg hearing. I turned on the super hearing and heard Daddy say that it might give me incentive to try harder with my schoolwork.

"Maybe," Mommy said. "But I'm still worried about the part about helping other kids because it might lead to dangerous situations."

"I doubt it," Daddy said. "I think it would be more like playing than anything, and it would only be with kids at the playground. It's not like he would be going out in the streets trying to catch real criminals. Besides, there's probably a way to monitor him because he seems to have Internet access. Maybe there's an app for parents of cyborg kids that we could download."

My hearing was so powerful that I heard Mommy roll her eyes.

"Well, there is a company that made his disguise," Daddy said. "And if they don't make an app, we can use the one I have that links my computer to the video camera on my phone." I knew what he meant because when Parker and I play in the backyard, he puts his phone out there with us so he can watch us from his computer.

Mommy didn't say anything, but I heard a slight noise that sounded like electric currents. Mommy was thinking about it!

"Besides," Daddy said. "It might help with his confidence. That's one of the most important things you can have, but it's not something you can teach. He seems more confident already."

"I guess we can give it a try," Mommy said, "as long as it doesn't interfere with schoolwork or cause any other problems. But if it becomes even the slightest bit dangerous or too much of a distraction, we end it and take him right down to Sven's Garage."

At this point I could no longer hold in my excitement. I burst into the kitchen and promised that I would do all my homework without complaining and stay at the playground and not get into any dangerous situations.

"Could you hear us the whole time?" Mommy asked me.

"Yes," I said.

"Tell your computer that you can't eavesdrop on your Daddy and Mommy," Daddy said. Before I could say anything else, a message appeared on my screen:

PARENT EAVESDROP RULE CREATED.

A few seconds later, Mommy and Daddy both received text messages on their phones that said the same thing.

"Wow!" Daddy said. "Can you create some rules about being HyperKid? Like making sure all of your homework is done and staying only at the playground and setting up a monitoring app we can use on our computers and..."

For the next several minutes Daddy started making up all sorts of crazy rules, including what to do when I encounter hostile aliens, ghosts, zombies, and rabid raccoons that had appetites for eating kids' homework. While he was talking, a message appeared on my screen that said "PROCESSING...". When Daddy was finally finished, Mommy added a few rules, including setting up warning messages and signals for potentially dangerous situations and restricting my abilities so that they couldn't seriously hurt someone unless it was a known kidnapper, predator, or wanted criminal. If a known kidnapper, predator, or wanted criminal came near me, a call would automatically be placed to 911 with my GPS coordinates, and Mommy and Daddy would immediately receive warning messages on all of their devices.

After they were finally done making up their crazy rules, they were both sent an email message titled "HyperKid Guidelines". The guidelines included all of Mommy and Daddy's rules and also a bunch of other stuff explaining everything else that had set up for them regarding my HyperKid activity.

"Wow!" Daddy said. "This is pretty impressive. It says here that after your homework is finished, your HyperKid mode will be switched on. At that point, if a kid needs help that is not a medical or crime-related situation, you will get a message and the navigation system will guide you to where the trouble is if it determines that you can help address the situation and still make it home in time for dinner. It also says that if the situation becomes potentially dangerous, we will be notified immediately, and the police will be notified if the danger becomes imminent. We will also have a live video stream that can be accessed through our phone or computer to see everything that is happening in real time, and everything will be recorded for legal and recreational purposes. Your location will be tracked using GPS so that we will know your exact location at all times, and there is also a parent recall feature that will command you to return home immediately if Mommy or Daddy activates it. And here are the links to the apps... hey, this is awesome!"

"There's also some kind of warranty," Mommy said. "If something goes wrong with your software or hardware, you can go down to Sven's Garage and they will make the repairs free of charge."

"Son, I always knew you would be a real super hero someday," Daddy said proudly. Mommy rolled her eyes again because she always said that there was no such thing as real super heroes like the ones in movies and video games. But now Daddy and I knew for sure that there were and that I was now one of them, so he held up his hand and I gave him a high five with my cyborg hand.

CHAPTER 5

The next morning there was a box waiting on the porch from the Shanghai SuperTech Corp, and inside was the new customized mask and glove. They fit perfectly and made me look exactly like my regular self except for a barely visible outline of the mask that you could only see if you looked really really close. Mommy said that if someone was close enough to my face to see the line, then they were too close anyway because they would be violating my personal space, which she always reminded me not to do to other people. I was glad that I could still be my regular self, but I was more excited that I could now disguise my secret identity like a real super hero.

It was Saturday, so after breakfast Mommy went upstairs to her sewing room and started working on my costume while Daddy and I started designing the HyperKid logo on his computer. I wasn't very good at drawing or handwriting, but I always liked creating super hero characters on video games and designing stuff on the computer, so this was right up my alley.

When it was finished, we printed the image on a special fabric paper and Mommy sewed it onto the costume. The main body of the costume was orange with yellow streaks of lightning (I wanted orange and yellow because it was the colors of fire), and the cape was black. Daddy mentioned that a lot of super heroes these days were going without capes, but I was a more of a traditionalist when it came to costume design and decided to keep it. Mommy also made a mask that covered most of my head and face to protect my identity.

When the costume was finally finished and I tried it on, I looked at myself in the mirror and couldn't believe it was really me. The red cyborg eye glowing through the hole of the mask looked truly awesome. Mommy and Daddy always said that I had special talents and abilities that I hadn't yet discovered, but I had no idea something like this could ever happen to a kid like me.

"You do understand that this isn't what makes you special," Daddy said. "You were already special, and you still have talents that are yours that you still haven't discovered yet. This super hero thing is just something wild and crazy that happened."

"And the coolest thing that ever happened," I said. "I want to be the greatest real life super hero ever!"

"We'll see about that," Mommy said. I could tell that she was still worried, but I would show her how awesome this was going to be. I was already starting to feel different because I now believed in myself. Daddy was always saying things like *you have to believe that you can do something before you can actually do it,* and *if you don't believe you can do something, then you won't be able do it*—blah blah blah—and for the first time in my life I knew what he meant. I truly believed that I could be a good super hero. I usually don't feel this way about doing my homework or swimming or riding a bicycle or pretty much anything besides playing with toys or video games. But I knew that I could be a good super hero, and I told Mommy and Daddy exactly that.

"You see," Daddy said. "That's what I'm talking about! If you also felt that way about doing your homework, then that would seem much easier too. And if you felt that way about *blah blah blah, blah blah, blah blah blah blah, blah blah blah blah blah blah blah blah blah…*"

Mommy says it would be hard for even the most focused and attentive person in the world to listen to someone talk as much as Daddy does sometimes.

CHAPTER 6

I spent the last couple of weeks of summer vacation testing my new super powers. I had super speed, super strength, and was able to jump about five feet in the air, but unfortunately I didn't have the big one: the ability to fly.

I also discovered that I was now really good at sports, which I never was before— especially tennis, which I hated with a passion because in gym class I always swung and missed and felt totally embarrassed. I knew Daddy would appreciate my new athletic talents because he is always watching sports on TV, so one day I asked him if he wanted to play baseball with me. He was very surprised because I usually said no whenever he asked if

I wanted to play any kind of sports, and he was happy because baseball was his favorite.

We grabbed a bat and some brand new baseballs that Daddy had bought for me a long time ago and walked down the road to the baseball field at my school. Daddy said that I could be up first and that he would pitch nice and slow for me. He stood on the pitcher's mound and leaned forward while holding the ball behind his back like the professional players do. He started shaking his head and nodding, then walked in a circle and kicked the dirt a few times, then started spitting on the grass (which was really gross), then got ready to pitch again before doing the same routine all over again.

"What are you doing?" I asked.

"Just making it more realistic like a big league pitcher," he said.

He got ready again, and this time he actually threw a pitch. As the ball approached, it felt like time had suddenly slowed down as my cyborg vision scanned the ball and locked a target on it. Before I realized what was happening, I swung the bat and hit the ball so hard that the cover came off and started falling towards the infield dirt while the inside of the ball kept going and eventually disappeared as it approached downtown. While the ball cover was still falling, I was running at hyper speed around the bases and made it back to home plate just before it landed.

This time it was Daddy's turn to faint in disbelief, so I picked up the bottle of water we had brought and poured it on his face.

"What happened?" Daddy asked when he came to.

"I think I hit a home run."

"Wow," he said. "I didn't even see where it landed. And I didn't even see you run around the bases. All I saw was dust!"

"Let's go home," I said.

"Have you reconsidered playing baseball on a team?" Daddy asked.

"No, I still don't want to join Little League."

"I'm not talking about Little League. I was thinking more like the New York Mets."

"Nah," I said.

"You'll probably make a lot more money than we're paying you in allowance. Hundreds of millions of dollars, probably."

"But our house isn't big enough for all the toys I would buy if I had that much money."

"That's a good point," Daddy said. "We have enough toys in the house. No more toys."

CHAPTER 7

Speaking of toys, Mommy and Daddy were always stepping on the toys that Parker and I left on the floor, but now my new cyborg

powers allowed me to clean them in record time. My new powers also enabled me to become a master at video games. I even beat Daddy's all-time high scores on his old arcade

games, which kind of depressed him because he was no longer able to wear his beat up old "King of the Arcade" T-shirt that he's had since he was a teenager.

Unfortunately, I also discovered that my new powers had their limits. A week before school started, Mommy and Daddy made me start doing some "refresher" reading, writing, and math work to get me back into school mode. At first I was actually excited about it because I thought it would be easy like so many other things had now become, but it was no different than before. My handwriting was still sloppy; I was still making lots of spelling errors; and I still had to count with my fingers for addition and subtraction problems.

During the second night of this "refresher" homework, I became so frustrated that I threw my pencil on the floor and screamed. Mommy and Daddy made me sit in the time out chair, and I started crying. I cried for a long time. When I finally calmed down long enough to talk, they asked why I was so upset.

"Because this was supposed to be easy!" I said, feeling like I was about to start crying again. "I thought that now that I had these new powers that all my schoolwork would be easy and I could just finish it quickly and get it over with. But it's still too hard!"

"It's not supposed to be easy," Mommy said. "You still have to work hard and practice to become good at things. Even with your new powers, there are still going to be things that are difficult to do. When you come across these things, all you can do is try your best. And even if you do something and it isn't perfect, or even if it's not good at all, the important part is whether or not you tried your best."

"But what if I fail?" I asked. "Failing is bad!"

"Not if you try your best," Daddy said. "And failures aren't always as bad as they seem. They can be opportunities. They can help you figure out what you need to work on and help you figure out what to do differently the next time you come across those same challenges. They can also help you figure out what you like and don't like, which is helpful in figuring out who you are and what you want to do with your life. As you get older, you will have to learn not to fear failure. You will certainly try to avoid it, and the most effective way to avoid it is to try your best at whatever you do—even if it's something you don't necessarily like to do, such as homework. But you can't be afraid of it, and you can't let it control you. If you truly try your best at everything you do—and I mean really, truly, honestly try—then failure won't find you very often. And when it does find you, it won't hurt so much because you'll know that you couldn't have possibly done anything more to succeed. That's all anyone can do, including the greatest super heroes."

I heard the *blah blah blah's* approaching in my mind, but I tried my best to listen so I could get out of the time out chair as soon as possible.

"Listen, bud," Daddy said, "You're also going to face some failures as a super hero. In fact, you're probably going to have all sorts of new problems. Being a super hero isn't easy. It's a huge responsibility. Even the best ones struggle sometimes. You're going to have to learn how to deal with these problems too."

"What kind of problems?" I asked.

"Well, the super heroes I've seen in the movies and in comic books aren't always the happiest people in the world. They all seem to have problems of some kind. Sometimes they feel lonely because they don't get to do all the things that regular people do. They can't just be themselves all the time because they have to keep secrets and wear disguises in order to protect themselves. It's not easy always having to hide who you truly are. You never feel free. You feel like you're in your own private prison. And people expect their heroes to be perfect all the time. You can save the day a million times, but if just one time you can't, people will start to turn on you. That level of responsibility can feel overwhelming."

"And super heroes also had to go to school when they were kids," Mommy said. "They had to learn how to write and spell and do math just like everyone else. Being a super hero does not excuse you from your regular responsibilities. You still have to be a normal fourth grader during the day. You can only be a super hero after school when you finish your homework."

"Harumph," I said.

CHAPTER 8

The first day of fourth grade was a nightmare.

First of all, our teacher, Mrs. Crabcake, assigned me the seat closest to her desk in the front of the classroom. This wouldn't have been so bad considering that I usually wind up in the front near the teacher's desk, but Mrs. Crabcake had long been rumored to be a sea monster. A half-human/half-kraken, to be exact, who had grown up in the deepest, darkest part of the ocean and was now over a thousand years old and counting. I had never even heard of a kraken until I first heard about Mrs. Crabcake way back in kindergarten, but it is apparently a giant octopus-like creature that swallows ships whole. Mrs. Crabcake is only half-kraken, though, so I guess the school board thinks it is safe for her to be around kids and is the reason why she is not bigger than a ship. A few weeks earlier when we received the teacher assignment letter in the mail, I told Mommy and Daddy about Mrs. Crabcake being half-kraken, but they said that rumors were not often true and that I should only believe proven facts. Mommy is a lawyer, so she went on about how they would have to test her DNA to prove it but doing so without being accused of committing a serious crime would violate her Constitutional rights, yet none of that mattered because krakens were mythical creatures anyway. Daddy disagreed with that last part and said that he had heard stories passed down from his Scandinavian ancestors that his great great great great great great grandfather was once on a ship that was swallowed whole by a kraken but that he managed to escape when it let out a big belch. Mommy said that this story was just a ridiculous old sea yarn, but Daddy insisted that it was true. Then Mommy told him to prove it, and they went back and forth for a while longer and didn't even notice when I left the room to play video games.

Anyway, I know that I'm never supposed to judge people by their appearance, and I know that I should get to know someone first before deciding how I feel about them, but this was a challenge with Mrs. Crabcake. She was unlike any human being I had ever encountered. She was a full-figured woman with long frizzy hair that made her head look like it was covered with seaweed, and she had a face like a wicked witch in a bad mood. Her face actually didn't look that old, but the granny glasses she wore made her appear older. Her long red fingernails looked like crab claws, and a huge crab pendant hung from her pearl necklace. Her dress was covered with images of seashells and starfish. While her appearance was unusual, it wouldn't have been so bad if she didn't smell like low tide on a hot summer afternoon.

I was so distracted by my fear that this woman might really be a sea monster disguised as a fourth grade teacher that I wasn't paying attention while she was calling everyone's name for attendance. She had to say my name three times before I heard her. The other kids laughed when I finally emerged from my trance and said "here". I was so embarrassed that I felt like screaming, but I managed to stay calm until the feeling passed. Mommy and Daddy say that taking slow deep breaths helps you stay calm, but it's hard to remember that when you're in the middle of a potential meltdown.

The most difficult part of school for me is sitting still and paying attention to the teacher instead of thinking about the ten million other things I'd rather be doing. If I had to sit still all day, at least I should be able to think about something fun like playing with my toys or video games, or playing with my toys and playing video games at the same time, or playing video games and with toys while watching a movie on my tablet. Daddy calls this "multi-tasking", which he says you should try to avoid because finishing one thing is better than not finishing two things. When you try to do two things at once, your mind will start battling itself over which thing to do. If you try to do both things at the same time, you'll get distracted and make mistakes or just feel overwhelmed to the point where you drop everything you're supposed to be doing and wind up doing something non-productive. Daddy also says that trying to do three or more things at once will tear the fabric of space-time and open a black hole that will swallow your world whole, so you should definitely stick to doing one thing at a time and remain focused on that until it is finished before moving on to the next thing.

After the attendance debacle, Mrs. Crabcake started going over her classroom rules, which seemed pretty straightforward until she said that absolutely no toys were allowed in her classroom.

"If I catch anyone with a toy in my classroom…" she began, but left the start of her warning hovering above us like a hawk waiting to strike. Her eyes were wide behind her granny glasses, and the room was so silent that it felt like time had come to a stop. Even my super hearing wasn't detecting any sounds beyond the slight whisper of the air being sucked out of the room. She then slid her granny glasses down her beaked nose as if to allow her beady black eyes to make direct contact with our fear. Suddenly those eyes locked onto me as if sensing my terror at the thought that my three favorite action figures—

Hot Dog Guy, Green Bean Man, and the villainous Trash Can Man—were stashed in the pocket of my backpack. We had not yet been assigned our cubbies, so the backpack was on the floor leaning against my leg. I was terrified because it felt like she was reading my mind. Normally when I'm scared I start to panic, but this level of fear was so intense that I was completely paralyzed. Finally, after what seemed like an eternity, she turned her attention to Robert sitting in the desk next to me with his finger in his nose and several boogers in his hair.

"If I catch anyone with a toy in my classroom," she repeated, "that toy will be taken away and not given back until the end of the school year in June."

If this ever happened, there would be no calm. Such a catastrophe would lead to the mother of all meltdowns. The longest timeout in the history of the world wouldn't be able to calm me down from that.

The tension finally eased when she began talking about school supplies. Fortunately she didn't notice the toys in my backpack as I carefully removed a few pencils from the side pocket and zipped it closed. I started to feel a little better knowing that if I didn't take the toys out for recess and just left them in my backpack all day, I should be able to get them back home safely.

Later that morning we had gym class. It was nice to get out of Mrs. Crabcake's classroom for a little while, but the gym teacher, Coach Skinnerd, said that we would be playing tennis.

As I mentioned earlier, I hate tennis. I didn't want to play, but I didn't want the new school year to get off to a bad start and risk a potential meltdown by whining like I did last year about how I hated tennis and didn't want to play. Coach Skinnerd was a big tough guy who acted like a drill sergeant, and he didn't go for that crying stuff. At the end of every class he always said, "Good job, men, now go hit the showers," even though our class had both boys and girls in it and the showers in the locker rooms hadn't been used in like 50 years.

The locker rooms themselves were pointless because elementary school kids don't change into gym clothes like they do in middle school and high school. Anyway, whenever something happened and I started crying, Coach Skinnerd would tell me to go hit the showers and then come back out and sit against the wall for the rest of class. So I would go into the boys locker room until I stopped crying, then come back out a few minutes later and take a seat on the floor next to the wall until class was over.

But I didn't want that to happen today, so I picked up the racket and waited my turn for Coach Skinnerd to lob the ball to me so that I could hit it back to him. I was so distracted by thinking about all the times I swung and missed last year that I forgot about my new cyborg powers. When it was my turn, he asked if I was ready. After I nodded, he lobbed the ball as slowly as he could. While it was floating towards me, my cyborg screen suddenly switched on and started targeting the ball like it had done at the baseball field with Daddy. After the target was locked, my arm swung the racket so fast that I didn't even feel it hit the ball.

Coach Skinnerd didn't have a chance to

react to the ball whizzing back towards him. It hit him square in the nose and shot off in a different direction. For a moment he was stunned like he didn't know what had just happened. I thought he was going to start yelling at me at any moment, but instead he fell backwards on his bottom and just sat there. The gym fell silent. For the second time that morning, it felt like time had come to a stop. Then a small stream of blood started trickling from his nose, which caused one of the other kids to gasp. I thought I was done for, but when he finally recovered from his shock and realized that his nose was bleeding, he made this horrible shrieking noise and started crying for his Mommy.

None of the other kids knew what to do. I was so scared that I was about to get in more trouble than I had ever been in my life that I fell to the floor and started crying uncontrollably. I usually cry whenever I accidentally hurt Parker or someone else, and Mommy and Daddy are always telling me that accidents sometimes happen and that I should make sure the person who got hurt is okay instead of worrying about getting in trouble. This thought did cross my mind, but I couldn't stop crying because this was Coach Skinnerd acting in a way that none of us had never seen before. He was normally a big tough guy who seemed invincible, but now that he wasn't being his usual self, we didn't know what he was going to do next. Through my tears I saw that some of the other kids also looked scared.

Finally, Gina, one of the girls in my class, said she would go to the nurse's office and tell Mrs. Stethoscope what had happened. After she was gone, a message started blinking on my cyborg screen:

STAY CALM

Unfortunately, this was not enough. Nor was the recording of Daddy's voice that the cyborg computer started playing in my head that thankfully only I could hear because he attempted to sound like a certain deep-voiced loud-breathing black-helmeted villain from an enormously popular movie franchise:

Is this thing on? Morgan, this is your father. Stay calm, my son. The situation will be easier to resolve if you remain calm… is that all I'm supposed to read? Can I also remind him not to pick at his lips and to make sure he brings all of his homework home? What was that? You want me to stick to the script? Okay. Stay calm, my son. Father out.

I have a nervous habit of picking at my lips because my hands are always looking for something to do, but at the moment I was too upset to even be doing that. I thought for sure that I would be going to go to jail for the rest of my life, and if they didn't let you have toys in fourth grade, they surely wouldn't let you have them in jail.

When Mrs. Stethoscope arrived, she saw me crying and came over to me first. The other kids started saying "over there" while pointing to Coach Skinnerd, who was now lying on his back pinching his nose and whimpering, but she stayed with me for a minute to make sure that I was okay and then told me to go to her office to calm down. Mrs. Stethoscope was really nice and was usually able to calm me down quickly whenever I had a meltdown at school. I even had a special chair in her office that I sat in to calm down. It didn't look any different than the other chairs, but she said it had special calming powers for kids like me. I knew it did because it worked every time.

As usual, the chair worked after a few minutes, but then I got upset all over again when it occurred to me that Mommy and Daddy might now change their minds about letting me keep my cyborg powers if they found out what happened. It wasn't even lunchtime of the first day of school and I had already taken out a teacher.

When Mrs. Stethoscope came back a few minutes later, I couldn't hold it in any longer and started crying again. She asked why I was so upset, so I told her that Coach Skinnerd was probably going to yell at me and call Mommy and Daddy and that I would be in a world of trouble. But Mrs. Stethoscope said that this was not going to happen because it was an accident, and that Coach Skinnerd was fine except that he sometimes acted like a big baby whenever he got a boo-boo. This made me laugh, and then she told me that when Coach

Skinnerd's nose had stopped bleeding, he asked where I was and wondered if I would be interested in joining the varsity tennis team. I didn't know what 'varsity' meant, but I said no because I didn't want to play tennis any more than I had to.

By recess I was feeling better and having fun on the playground until I saw one of my friends who had been in my third grade class, Johnny J. Johnson. I was sad that Johnny wasn't in my class this year, but what really got me was that he was holding his Slime Bucket Man action figure right out in the open.

"Aren't you worried that your teacher might take it away?" I asked.

"Why?" he asked.

"Mrs. Crabcake doesn't let us have toys in the classroom. She said she would take them away until the end of the year if she even sees them."

"Mr. Cooldude said we can bring small toys like action figures to school," Johnny said. "He even said that we can play with them in the classroom if there's time after everyone finishes their work. Mr. Cooldude is the greatest teacher in the world!"

I thought I was going to have another meltdown. Mr. Cooldude really did sound like the greatest teacher in the world, while I was stuck with the rotten fish lady Mrs. Crabcake.

"It's too bad that we're not in the same class this year," Johnny said. "You would really like Mr. Cooldude. Hey, why don't you ask to switch into my class? I don't see why they wouldn't let you since it's still the first day."

The oncoming meltdown was suddenly derailed by this great ray of hope. After all, Johnny was right. It was still only the first day and we hadn't actually done any work yet—so why wouldn't they let me switch classes? I'm sure Mrs. Crabcake wouldn't mind since she didn't seem to like kids anyway, so having one less in her classroom should seem agreeable to her. For the first time ever, I couldn't wait for recess to be over so that I could ask her if I could switch into Mr. Cooldude's class.

But when we got back to the classroom after recess, Mrs. Crabcake wasn't there. After sitting at our desks for a few minutes, we started growing restless. I heard one of the other kids whisper that maybe she wouldn't come back and that we would get a new teacher. This would have been great except that I really wanted to be in Mr. Cooldude's class. While anyone would have been better than Mrs. Crabcake, it didn't seem likely that another teacher would let us play with toys in the classroom.

After a few more minutes, the buzz in the classroom had reached fever pitch. Maybe she really wasn't coming back. Maybe she had returned to the bottom of the sea and the principal was scrambling to find a replacement. Maybe they would split us up into the other fourth grade classes and they were just trying to figure out who would go where. Maybe I would wind up in Mr. Cooldude's class after all!

Finally, a chorus of moans signaled that our hopes and dreams had been crushed when Mrs. Crabcake walked in through the open classroom door. But the moans quickly turned to gasps when we saw that she was not alone.

With her was a boy who must have been the biggest fourth grader in the world—if in fact he really was a fourth grader. His hair was messy like he hadn't bathed in weeks. His jeans were ripped, but not fashionably ripped like the high school kids—it looked more like he had been attacked by a badger. The sleeves had been torn off his unbuttoned flannel shirt, and underneath he wore a printed t-shirt featuring the skull of a bull's head with a nose ring hanging from its nostrils. The kid's own nostrils flared like a real bull, and my super hearing picked up some slight grunting under his breath. His eyes were bloodshot, and his eyebrows were furrowed like he was ready to strike. His fists were stuffed in the pockets of his jeans. His shoelaces were untied.

"This is our new student, Brian Bullini," Mrs. Crabcake announced. "He just transferred to us from East Plains. Everyone, say hello to Brian and make him feel welcome."

"Call me Bull," he grunted. His voice sounded almost as deep as Daddy's.

"In this classroom, you will be known as 'Brian'," Mrs. Crabcake said. A few of the other kids laughed nervously, but the room instantly fell back to stunned silence when Bull scowled at us.

By now I had already forgotten about asking Mrs. Crabcake if I could transfer into Mr. Cooldude's class. I could tell by the expressions of shock and horror around the room that we were all thinking the same thing.

Everyone had heard the stories about East Plains kids—that they are actually alien zombies with three eyes and tails and webbed feet disguised as regular kids; that they eat bugs for breakfast, mud pies made of real mud for dessert, and use their glowing green snot as syrup on their pancakes; that their hair is actually poison vines that would paralyze you if you ever touched it; and that if you look at East Plains kids directly in their eyes, they go into super-psycho zombie mode and eat you.

This was the first time I had knowingly seen an East Plains kid up close. While this Brian Bullini wasn't exactly what I had imagined an East Plains kid would look like, my cyborg sensors started scanning him and a message appeared on my screen:

```
***CYBORG DETECTED***

METEOR TYPE:  RED
POWERS:  CONFIRMED

PROFILE:  BRIAN BULLINI, A.K.A. "BULL THE
BULLY", FORMERLY OF EAST PLAINS BUT
NOW RESIDING IN WEST PLAINS. CURRENTLY
WEARING CUSTOMIZED MASK AND GLOVE
FROM SHANGHAI SUPERTECH CORP.

***BEWARE***
```

I didn't know that "a.k.a." meant "also known as" until I asked Daddy about it later, but I did know that I was a green meteor type and I also knew about the Shanghai SuperTech Corp. I realized that he must have been exposed to meteor rays like I had been, except his were red and mine were green. In the super hero world, green usually meant good and red usually meant bad.

But what really made me nervous was that he suddenly started staring directly at me as if his sensors detected that I was a cyborg as well. This meant that he now probably knew as much about me as I knew about him. I also knew that he might very well be my first arch enemy as a super hero.

Daddy was right. Super heroes do have extra stuff to worry about that other people don't.

CHAPTER 9

Mrs. Crabcake sent us home with what she said was a month's worth of homework and a schedule of assignments that we were supposed to do each night, but the piles of books and worksheets seemed like enough homework to last through middle school. We had to do three pages of math a night, read two essays, and then write a summary and answer questions about each essay. And that doesn't even include the twenty minutes of mandatory independent reading we had to do every night from the book of our choice, which we also had to write brief summaries for.

This was ridiculous, unfair, unjust, and just plain mean. It also didn't help that I was having more difficulty than usual focusing on my homework because it was the first official day of my super hero career as HyperKid. I had to be ready to jump into action in case someone needed my help. I also had to watch out for my possible arch enemy, which is what I was most worried about.

Daddy worked from home during the day and Mommy worked in the big city, so Daddy helped with my homework after school and made dinner for Parker and I in the evening. After my long first day I was kind of tired and out of practice for doing homework, so it took longer than it should have and about halfway through I had a bit of a meltdown. I told Daddy that this was too much and that I wanted to transfer to Mr. Cooldude's class, but instead of agreeing with me like he should have, he started talking about lemons and how if life gives them to me I should make lemonade. This sounded good because it had been a long hot day, so I asked if I could have some lemonade, but he said that it was just an expression meant to teach me how to make the best of difficult situations. So I said that we should make the best of this difficult situation by making lemonade, but Daddy said that we didn't have any lemons or lemonade mix, which made me even more upset because now

I really wanted lemonade.

After a long time out, I finally managed to finish the rest of my homework. As soon as I put my pencil down, a message appeared on my cyborg screen:

BULLY ALERT
WEST PLAINS ELEMENTARY PLAYGROUND
RED METEOR CYBORG PRESENCE DETECTED
BULLY ACTIVITY REPORTED

I told Daddy about the alert and he said that he received the same one on his phone and that I could go. I ran upstairs, put my costume on, and ran back downstairs, but Daddy stopped me before I got to the door. He was having one of his mushy proud parent moments and wanted to take my picture and started talking about how he couldn't believe his little boy had grown up to be a super hero *blah blah blah*. It looked like he was about to start crying, but I had a job to do so I used my super speed to run around him and out the door before he even realized what was happening.

Fortunately the school was only two blocks away, so I was there in a matter of seconds. When I arrived at the scene, I heard Daddy's voice through my cyborg communication system and he told me to be careful and that he was watching me on his computer. My system was equipped with GPS, which basically meant that Mommy and Daddy could tell where I was at all times and could track my movements through an app on their phones and computers. Daddy also asked what I wanted for dinner and I told him chicken nuggets and green beans with apple sauce.

Just outside the playground there were several kids on their way home, a couple of them in tears and one of them crying for his mommy. I asked a fleeing girl what had happened, and she pointed towards the swings inside the playground.

And there he was. Brian Bullini, a.k.a. Brian the Bull, a.k.a. Bull the Bully, a.k.a. HyperKid's arch enemy. He was standing near the swings with arms folded and laughing with a loud bully laugh that echoed against the brick walls of the school building, across the ball fields, and all throughout the rest of West Plains. I had heard the laugh from all the way back home, but I didn't realize what the sound was until now.

Now I was really scared, especially when Bull noticed me approaching.

"Nice pajamas, kid!" he said loudly. "Did your Mommy make them for you?"

He then did his loud bully laugh again, which made me really mad. I was so mad that I wasn't even nervous anymore. My cyborg systems must have sensed this because a message appeared on my screen that said STAY CALM, and then Daddy said it too.

"He's just trying to get you mad," Daddy said. "Remember, sticks and stones may break your bones, but words can never give you a boo-boo. Or a flesh wound. Or one of those bruises that's purple in the middle and brown around the outside. Just ask him what he did to the other kids."

"What did you do to the other kids?" I asked softly.

"Did you say something, Underpants Boy?" Bull said and laughed.

"Louder!" Daddy said. "Say it like Hot Dog Guy would, with confidence and louder than your regular voice, but not yelling or angry."

"I'm talking to you, Underpants Boy!" Bull said and laughed again.

"Ask him again, loudly, now!" Daddy said, but there was too much happening at once and I started to panic. I didn't know what to do. I just wanted to run and hide, so I turned around and ran back home. When I got there I ran up to my room and buried myself under the blankets and started crying.

I heard Daddy coming up the stairs and I knew he was going to want to talk. But I didn't want to talk, I just needed a hug. And he must have known this because he didn't say anything when he came in my room, he just lifted the blankets off and hugged me.

I was able to calm down after a few minutes and sat up next to him.

"What happened, bud?" he asked.

"I got scared," I said. I felt like I was going

to start crying again just thinking about it. "I didn't know what to do."

"I was scared too," Daddy said. "I saw the whole thing."

"He's the new kid in my class," I said. "And he's a cyborg too. A red meteor cyborg. Do you know what that means?"

Daddy thought about it for a moment. "I'm not really sure," he said. "I don't know much about cyborgs... or meteors."

"I think it means he's a bad guy cyborg," I said. "I'm a green meteor type, which means I'm a good guy."

"Well, we know that you're a good guy, but we don't know for sure yet that he's a bad guy," Daddy said. "You can't tell by looking at someone that they're a bad guy, and we don't yet know what these meteor colors mean."

"But my cyborg screen said that it was a bully alert! And then he scared the kids away on the playground! And then he made fun of me and called me 'Underpants Boy'!"

"I heard what he called you, and that wasn't nice," Daddy said. "As for your bully alert, we don't know how trustworthy it is at this point. Maybe your cyborg system has a rivalry with his cyborg system that has nothing to do with either of you. We just don't know.

"And we don't know what happened with the other kids at the playground before you got there. They might have been scared of him as soon as they saw him and started running away because of the way he looks. That might have hurt his feelings, and maybe that's why he started being mean—if he really was being mean at all. Maybe the laughing was just a reaction to the other kids being mean to him.

"And maybe he's been going through stuff

like this his whole life. If he really is a bully, maybe it was others being mean to him that influenced it. Maybe things aren't so good with his family. Sure, part of his appearance is his fault because of the way he's dressed, including the shirt with the sleeves ripped off and the t-shirt with the scary bull skull. Considering that nobody here knows him yet, maybe this does make him seem scary to the other kids.

"But the part that's not his fault is that he's much bigger than the other kids in fourth grade. That alone makes him look different. Some people are scared of others who simply look different, and they decide not to like them without even getting to know them or giving them a chance to show who they really are. And that's not right.

"At this point we don't know Bull's whole story. All we know is that he just moved here from East Plains, and today was his first day at a new school. Being the new kid can be an extremely stressful and scary experience, especially when you know you look different than the other kids. If the kids back in East Plains were mean to him, he might just assume that the kids here will be mean to him too. That isn't right either. But he might be more scared of you and your classmates than you guys are of him, and that might cause him to act inappropriately. But you have to keep an open mind. He might not really be a bully. He might just be acting out because he's scared."

Daddy's speech was pretty convincing, but my cyborg sense wasn't totally buying it.

"I still think he's a bad guy," I said. "The warning message on my cyborg screen said that he was a.k.a. 'Bull the Bully' and that he was a red meteor type cyborg and to beware. And he grunted at us like a real bull and everyone in the class was scared. Then at the playground all the kids were leaving and one of them was crying, and when I asked that girl what happened, she pointed to Bull. And he's my arch enemy! All super heroes have arch enemies! So, if I'm a good guy and he's my arch enemy, that automatically makes him a bad guy."

"I see your point, but all of that is still circumstantial evidence," Daddy said.

"What does that mean?"

"It means that while what we know so far makes it look like he's guilty of being a bully, it still doesn't prove it. We don't even know if he's really your arch enemy."

"But he is! And he's from East Plains!"

"I know what they say about kids from East Plains," Daddy said. "They said the same things about East Plains kids when I was in fourth grade, and the kids over there say the same things about West Plains kids. That's just an old town rivalry between West Plains and East Plains. I have actually gotten to know a lot of people from East Plains over the years, and most of them are nice, normal people. I also know a few people from West Plains who aren't so nice. You can't judge people by where they come from or any other characteristic that lumps them together with a larger group of people. You should only judge a person after you get to know him or her as an individual."

Daddy paused as if he knew the *blah blah blahs* were coming.

"I have an idea," Daddy said. "Why don't you talk to him at school tomorrow? It's really difficult being the new kid, and he might just need someone to be nice to be him before he starts being nice to you guys. If nobody is nice to him, he's not going to be nice to anyone else."

"But I don't want to talk to him! I'm scared of him!"

"Like I said, he might be scared of you too."

"He called me 'Underpants Boy'!"

"I know, I know. But try to ignore that for now. Just say hello to him tomorrow and see what he does. If he's still not nice to you after that, then that's his fault. But if even one person is nice to him and makes him feel welcome, his whole attitude might change. That one simple gesture would be more heroic than confronting him on the playground later."

"I don't know if I still want to be a super hero if I have to do stuff like this," I said. "I just want to have the super powers."

"You should do stuff like this whether you're a super hero or not. You don't have to be a super hero to help someone, and you should always try to help someone if you can. If you told me right now that you didn't want to be HyperKid anymore, I would still want you to say hello to him tomorrow."

I was starting to feel exhausted.

"What if I don't say hello tomorrow?" I asked.

"I would be disappointed that you didn't do this one simple thing to try to help someone. "

"But Hot Dog Guy is never nice to Trash Can Man!"

"That's just pretend, bud," Daddy said. "If Hot Dog Guy had been nice to Trash Can Man, then Trash Can Man might have stopped stealing people's stuff and replacing it with garbage. Then you wouldn't have much of a good-versus-evil story and nobody would be interested in watching it, and then the studios would stop making it because they wouldn't be making any money from it. But that's just TV shows and movies and comic books.

"This is the real world. In the real world, you don't need super powers to be a hero. You just have to help someone by doing something that most other people *wouldn't* do—even though they probably could if they really tried.

"I'm willing to bet that most of your classmates won't say hello to him tomorrow. They could do it easily and it would take less than a second, but they probably won't. The ones who do say hello are the ones who have the best chance of being heroes by being brave enough to do something that others are afraid or just unwilling to do. I'm not saying that a simple *hello* will tame the Bull, but it might help him feel a little more welcome—and that's a start that might lead to a better situation for everyone. You'd be surprised what a powerful effect that simply being nice can have on a person, and also how good it can make you feel."

"I'm still too scared to say hello to him."

"Another part of being a hero is overcoming fear. Most of those other kids are probably just as afraid as you to say hello to him. But heroes are brave enough to overcome their fears to help someone else."

"I don't know how to be brave."

"You just have to try to stay focused on the one thing you have to do and block everything else out. Think of a firefighter running into a burning building to save someone. Obviously that is a scary thing, but that firefighter is so focused on saving the person inside that he or she is able to ignore their fear in order to save that person. The fear is still there, but saving the person is more important, so the firefighter is able to push the fear aside and say *Get out of my way, I have a person to save!*

"In your case, saying hello to Brian is the thing you need to focus on. If fear starts banging on the door trying to get in, ignore it. Don't let it in. If it breaks down the door, think of it as the one person you're allowed to be rude to. Tell it to shut up and go away. Call it a stinkbutt or a wimp or a doodyhead. Just don't let it control you. You're the boss of yourself, not some jerk like fear who is trying to stop you from doing something important.

"If all that doesn't work, just tell yourself that the sooner you say hello, the sooner your fear will go away simply because you won't have to think about it anymore. Just get it over with. Sometimes thinking about something is worse than actually doing it. If you don't say hello, you're just going to keep thinking about it and feeling afraid. You might also start to feel bad if no one else is nice to him. But I know you can do it, bud. And do you know what will happen right after you say hello?"

"What?"

"You'll begin to feel stronger as a person. And I'm talking about real strength, not artificial super hero strength. When you overcome a fear, you immediately begin to feel stronger. Then when fear shows up next time, it will be weaker and you will be stronger, and you'll be able to defeat it more easily. And if you keep defeating it, you'll start to feel confident that you can do just about anything because you know that fear isn't going to stand in your way. That is real power. Having confidence in yourself is more powerful than having super abilities.

"Even super heroes like Hot Dog Guy have to overcome their fears. He probably spent many long lonely hours working hard at developing his skills and facing his fears. But eventually he defeated his fears and became confident in his abilities. That's how he became so powerful."

"I don't remember that," I said.

"Well, maybe they'll show it in a prequel or an origin story reboot movie or something," Daddy said. "I think they picked up the storyline when he was already a powerful super hero.

"Anyway, some people never overcome their fears and miss out on many amazing experiences because of it, and then later in life they regret it. Quite often they realize that what they had been so afraid of actually wouldn't have hurt them so badly, or that there was actually nothing to be afraid of at all. They had let their fears defeat them for no real reason. They hadn't considered that the later regret of not doing it would be worse than whatever they were initially afraid of.

"There are times when you should feel afraid, like when you're in a situation when you or someone else could get hurt. But fear is often an exaggeration of your imagination, especially when you're young. Now I want you to ask yourself, *What's the worst thing that can happen if I say hello to Brian tomorrow morning?*"

"He might take out his cyborg blasters and shoot me," I said.

"Do you really think that would happen just for being nice and saying hello to him? Or would there be more of a chance of him blasting you later if you *don't* say hello to him? Sometimes the consequence of *not* doing something is worse than whatever it is you're afraid of. If he knows you're a cyborg and you don't say hello to him, he might see you as a rival or a threat, and that might put you and everyone else in danger. But if you do say hello, maybe he won't perceive you as a threat and will be less likely to attack you later."

In addition to my exhaustion, I was now starting to get a headache.

"Fine," I said, trying to sound as frustrated as I could so Daddy would know that I was not happy about taking his advice. "I'll say hello."

"Good," Daddy said. "I know this seems like the hard thing to do, and that it might seem easier *not* to say hello, but facing your fears and doing difficult things will make you a stronger person. Doing easy things all the time won't get you anywhere. Doing difficult things—even if you don't always succeed at them—is what will make you strong."

CHAPTER 10

When I got to school the next morning, Bull was already seated at his desk in the back of the room. He was staring out the window and I was relieved that he didn't seem to notice me walk in. I was terrified about what I had to do, yet I somehow managed to build enough courage to make the long walk to his desk.

I wasn't sure if I should call him "Bull" or "Brian", so I just said "Hi" with a quiet voice. For a moment he didn't react at all, but when he did finally look at me, I thought that he didn't look as scary as he did the day before. He actually looked kind of sad. I waited for him to say "hi" back, but after staring at me for a couple of seconds, he suddenly made a mean face and grunted under his breath. At that point I decided that my work was done, so I went to my desk and didn't look back at him for the rest of the morning.

At recess I assumed Bull would be busy scaring the other kids, which I thought might be a good thing because our school has a strict no bullying policy that would get him in trouble without me having to get involved. But he was just standing near the same spot where he had been scaring the kids the day before, only now he was leaning against the fence and looking down at the ground. Again he looked sad, even more so than earlier. I didn't know what to make of this, and neither did my cyborg system because I didn't receive any alerts about his presence.

Some of the other kids from my class were also watching him from a safe distance and were completely unaware that he had cyborg super hearing and might be listening to everything they were saying about him.

Gina said, "I heard that he got kicked out of East Plains Elementary because the kids and the teachers and even the principal were so scared of him that everyone stopped showing up for school, and it took the entire East Plains Police Department to get him out of the building, and then the Army showed up at his house with a hundred tanks to kick him and his family out, and if they ever step foot in East Plains again they will get arrested and spend the rest of their lives in jail."

Rhonda said, "He smells like a garbage truck because he hasn't taken a bath since he was in diapers."

"Stop telling mean lies about him," Sergio said to Gina and Rhonda. "The real reason he was kicked out of East Plains Elementary was that he isn't fully potty trained and that he poops in his pants all the time."

Gina and Rhonda looked at each other and laughed because Sergio was often called "Stinkbutt" behind his back for his occasional accidents.

I didn't know what to believe. But seeing him standing there all alone and knowing that he was probably hearing everything the other kids were saying actually made me feel bad for him. Suddenly I wasn't as afraid of him anymore, and I was no longer sure that he was really my arch enemy. In fact, it felt like I was more like Bull and less like these other West Plains kids. I didn't want him to think that I was mean like the other kids, so I started walking away from them and towards Bull.

I heard the other kids calling my name behind me and telling me to stay away, but I ignored them. Even my cyborg screen was blinking a warning message that said "CAUTION: BULL CYBORG SYSTEM HAS DETECTED YOUR DIRECT APPROACH", but I managed to make the message disappear by thinking the words "DELETE MESSAGE". I knew what I had to do. I was also determined not to let Bull scare me away again like he did the day before.

I stopped a few feet in front of him. I sniffed the air expecting to smell garbage, but I didn't smell anything. Bull looked up at me for a moment, but instead of scaring me away, he just looked back down at the ground without making any grunting noises or anything.

After Mrs. Crabcake's warning about bringing toys to school, I had originally decided that I was not going to risk them being taken away—especially my favorite ones. But this morning before school when I was still worried about saying hello to Bull, I decided that I needed to have them with me to remind me to be brave and hid two of them in my pants pockets. My cyborg system gave me a warning message about bringing toys to school, but I just deleted it knowing that I had to have them with me if I was going to pull this off. I just had to be extremely careful not to let Mrs. Crabcake see them.

Now I reached into my pockets and pulled out the two action figures—Hot Dog Guy, and the villainous Gasbag Man, who farted his enemies into submission—and held them out for Bull to see.

"Do you want to play with me?" I asked.

Bull didn't look up, but this time he grunted. The sound made me realize that I sometimes grunted too when Mommy and Daddy asked me annoying questions like how school was or if had put soap on the washcloth or if I wanted green beans or broccoli with my dinner when they already know that I can't stand broccoli.

"Go away," he finally mumbled. I heard Gina calling me from across the playground saying that Mrs. Crabby-Pants was going to take my toys away if she knew I had them, but I ignored her.

"I'll be Hot Dog Guy if you want to be Gasbag Man," I said.

He just grunted again, so I put the toys back in my pocket and started walking away but stopped when he grunted again.

"I want Hot Dog Guy," he growled.

I couldn't believe it. I thought for sure that that Bull would want to play with the villain rather than the fun-loving silly super hero who has an endless appetite for frankfurters. Hot Dog Guy was my favorite all-time super hero and this was my favorite toy, so I didn't want to let Bull have him. But he was looking at me like he was hoping I would say yes, and I didn't want him to feel sad again.

"Okay," I finally said, then held Hot Dog Guy out for him to take.

Suddenly he looked up, smiled, and grabbed Hot Dog Guy from my hand. But instead of starting to play, he put the action figure in his pocket and said, "Thanks, Underpants Boy," and walked away.

I thought for sure that I was going to start

crying. Having my favorite toy taken away was one of my greatest fears. But, to my own amazement, I stayed calm. My back was turned to the other kids, but I knew they had probably seen the whole thing. This was confirmed when I turned around to see Gina confront Bull and yell at him to give it back, but he responded by roaring at her with a face that could scare the moon away from Earth. Gina then screamed so loudly that the kids standing near her covered their ears. It was not unusual for Gina to scream because she screamed all the time about anything, like getting less than 100% on a test or if she sneezed or if it was raining. But when Bull responded to her scream with the same loud bully laugh he had done the day before, my calm quickly turned into a rage like I had never felt before.

I felt my fists clench tight, and I was about to run after him and attack with all my cyborg might until a message appeared on my screen:

STAY CALM... CYBORG POWERS DEACTIVATED... STAY CALM...

I turned around expecting to see Bull walking away, but all I saw was the other kids running to line up. Bull was nowhere in sight.

Since my cyborg system was offline, I couldn't use the GPS tracker to locate him. I began running towards the lineup area hoping to spot him from there, but I still didn't see him. I felt a major panic attack coming on as I began to realize that I may never get Hot Dog Guy back. I couldn't tell Mrs. Crabcake about it because she would just say that I wasn't supposed to have toys in school, and Mommy and Daddy would probably say the same thing. This was too much for me to handle. When I got to our class line I still didn't see Bull anywhere. I started feeling feverish. I was going to ask the other kids if they had seen him, but I started gagging and couldn't get the words out. Then, before I could to get to a less crowded spot, I threw up all over Gina's shoes.

Gina, of course, started screaming in horror. One of the teachers came over and saw what had happened and told me to go to the nurse's office. Gina continued screaming while I was walking away, and I could still hear her even when I was inside the building. By the time I got to the nurse's office I couldn't hold it in anymore and started crying.

Mrs. Stethoscope led me to my special chair. After a few minutes I was able to calm down enough to tell her what had happened, and then she took my temperature.

"You have a slight fever, but it's nothing serious," she said. "I think you just caught the stomach bug that's been going around. You'll probably be fine by tomorrow, but I'm going to send you home."

Normally being sent home by the nurse would be a joyous occasion, but not today. I would be leaving school without Hot Dog Guy, and it now seemed like a sure thing that I would never see him again. I was also worried that Daddy would be upset because I had brought toys to school when I wasn't supposed to until it occurred to me that he didn't know that this is what caused me to get sick. As far as he knew, I had just caught a stomach bug. But that wasn't making me feel any better.

Daddy said I didn't look too good when he picked me up. When we got back home, he gave me some fever reducing medicine and asked how I was feeling.

"Not good," I said. Then I started crying.

"It's probably just a little stomach virus," he said. "You'll start to feel better in a little while when that medicine kicks in."

"That's not why I'm crying!"

While I knew that Daddy wouldn't be happy about me sneaking a toy to school, I also knew that I had to tell him if I was to have any chance of ever getting Hot Dog Guy back. To my surprise, though, he wasn't upset at all.

"I'm proud of you, bud," he said. "You went out of your way and risked your favorite toy to be nice to this kid, and then you had the courage to tell me the truth even though you were worried that you would get in trouble. That's heroic. Unfortunately, this guy acted like a real jerk."

"I want Hot Dog Guy back!" I cried.

"We'll get Hot Dog Guy back," Daddy said. "And if not, I'll buy you a new one. But I think this is a job for… HyperKid!"

CHAPTER 11

Even though I had been sent home by the nurse, Daddy understood that I wasn't really sick and allowed me to go to the playground after I finished my homework to see if Bull was there with my Hot Dog Guy.

I was very nervous and walked at regular speed to get there. While I really wanted Hot Dog Guy back, part of me was hoping that Bull wouldn't be there because I didn't want to be reminded of what had happened earlier. I was also afraid of whatever he might do next. This guy was bad news.

The playground was completely empty, which was a strange sight on such a nice fall afternoon. I thought that Bull may have already scared the kids away and gone home because his bullying work was done for the day.

I entered the playground and looked around. I didn't see anything at first, and after a few minutes I was about to go back home when something caught my eye. There, on the seat of one of the swings, was what looked like an action figure. When I got closer I couldn't believe what I was seeing—it was Hot Dog Guy! I started running towards him, but suddenly there was a roar so loud that I fell down.

When I looked up I saw something so unbelievable that I didn't know what to think. It was Bull wearing his own super hero costume, except his was a hodgepodge of mismatched items that made it difficult to tell whether he was trying to look like a super hero or a cyborg clown. Only the yellow dish towel cape and the big letter "B" with bull horns drawn sloppily on the front enabled him to pull off the super hero look. An old knit cap with eye holes cut out was pulled all the way down to the bottom of his nose. Through the eye hole on his right, his exposed cyborg eye glowed bright red and was a terribly frightening sight even though it looked exactly like mine. On his left hand he wore a glove from an old space ranger costume similar to the one I had worn on Halloween when I was in kindergarten. His right cyborg hand was uncovered and looked just like mine. His legs were covered with tight space ranger pajama pants that were several sizes too small and reached only to his knees, and his feet were covered with a dirty old pair of rubber rain boots.

"Halt in the name of justice, Underpants Boy," he said.

"My name is not Underpants Boy," I said, feeling the anger flaring up inside me again. I stood up and brushed the dirt and grass off my legs "My name is HyperKid."

Bull laughed out loud.

"Who are you supposed to be?" I asked.

"I am BullBorg," he said triumphantly.

I was tempted to ask if his Mommy had made that costume for him in the same mean way he had asked me the day before, but that didn't seem like the right thing to do. I actually felt kind of bad that his mommy obviously didn't make a really cool costume for him like mine had made for me.

"I just came to get my Hot Dog Guy back," I said. "I see him on the swing over there."

"Hot Dog Guy, you say? Why, he's my sidekick now!"

"But he's a good guy," I said. "And you're a villain!"

I was expecting the heated exchange to continue, but instead BullBorg just looked down at his boots and said nothing. Then I heard a noise that was very familiar to me but completely unexpected coming from him. It sounded like he was crying.

"Why are you crying?" I asked.

"I'm not crying!" BullBorg shouted, but clearly he was. "I'm a good guy! I'm not a villain!"

"But you took my toy!" I said. "Why would you take my toy if you're a good guy?"

"Because Hot Dog Guy is the perfect sidekick for a good guy hero like me!"

"Then why don't you get your own Hot Dog Guy?"

To this he did not answer but started crying again.

"I just want my toy back," I said, looking at Hot Dog Guy standing triumphantly on the seat of the swing.

"No!" BullBorg yelled. "You can't have him!" He then pointed his cyborg index finger at me and shot a laser beam that struck the "H" logo on my chest and sent me reeling backwards a few feet, but it wasn't powerful enough to knock me down. Before I realized what I was doing, I pointed my cyborg index finger back at him and shot a more powerful laser beam that struck him right on the "B". He reeled backwards a few feet and fell hard on his butt and then on his back.

For a long moment he didn't move. I became worried that he was seriously injured, but then he suddenly jumped to his feet and ran towards the gate on the far side of the ball fields. With my super hearing I heard him crying as he ran. I stood and watched as he passed through the gate and disappeared into the neighborhood.

I retrieved my Hot Dog Guy from the swing and looked at him. As much as I loved this toy, I wasn't as happy as I thought I would be to have it back.

Daddy was waiting for me when I got home. I thought for sure he was going to be mad about me shooting BullBorg with my laser, but instead he gave me a hug and asked if I was okay, which I was. His laser hadn't hurt me, and Daddy said it was okay that I used mine because I was defending myself, which is the only time I should use it. He also said that my lasers are only powerful enough to stun someone and possibly knock them over, but not to seriously hurt them.

After we were done talking, I went back upstairs and changed into my civilian clothes. Then I put Hot Dog Guy next to my backpack so that I would remember to bring him to school the next morning and give him to Bull for keeps.

CHAPTER 12

The next day, however, Bull was not at school. After finishing my homework that afternoon, I went down to the playground dressed in my civilian clothes with Hot Dog Guy in my pocket, but there was still no sign of Bull. A few kids were there, which probably meant that he hadn't been around at all today.

The following day was Friday, and again Bull wasn't at school or at the playground. I was beginning to think that maybe he had moved again and was gone for good when a message appeared on my cyborg screen:

INCOMING MESSAGE FROM BULLBORG:

HI HYPERKID! DO YOU WANT TO COME OVER TO MY HOUSE TO PLAY?

I told Daddy about the message, and he was surprised that Bull invited me to come over. He was also surprised that I would even consider going over there after all that had happened. Then I told him that I wanted to give Hot Dog Guy to Bull, which surprised him even more. But he said he still wasn't so sure that it was a good idea to go over there, and besides, we didn't know where he lived anyway. But as soon as Daddy had finished saying that, he got a text message that said it was from HyperKid. The message had Bull's home address and step-by-step directions of how to get there.

"How did you do that so fast?" Daddy asked.

"I don't know," I said, laughing in disbelief. "I didn't even know that I was sending you a message!"

"Well, I suppose I can drive you over there," he said. "He lives a few miles away. But I'm not going to let you stay there by yourself. I want to meet his parents before anything else. And we have to take Parker with us because Mommy is still at work."

With me sitting next to Parker in our usual spots in the back seat (he still sat in a booster seat), Daddy drove through downtown, past the train station, and into a part of West Plains that I had never seen before. The houses around here looked really old, and some of them were falling apart. There were also some properties where houses probably used to stand that were now vacant lots filled with trash. There was also a lot of litter on the sidewalks, and most of the front yards were overgrown with weeds. The few houses that didn't look so bad had tall iron gates surrounding them. It was scary to think that people actually lived around here because it looked like a scene from a scary movie.

Eventually Daddy turned down a dead end road where there were houses on one side and a big auto junkyard on the other. We drove slowly all the way down to the very last house before stopping.

"There's his house," Daddy said. "But I don't know about this, bud. This isn't a very nice neighborhood."

I was kind of scared myself, but I had already sent a message to Bull saying that I would come over. Daddy turned the car around and parked facing in the direction we had just come from.

"Just in case we have to make a quick getaway," he said with a nervous laugh.

The house looked empty until I noticed Bull's red cyborg eye peeking out at us through the blinds of the front porch window. My cyborg screen then put up a message that said "CAUTION: BULLBORG."

"I don't know if I want you to get out of the car," Daddy said.

"Don't worry," I said. "If anything happens, I'll just use my blasters."

"Okay," Daddy said. "You can go knock on the door, but I don't want you to go inside. When he answers the door, ask him if he can get one of his parents to come out so I can talk to them."

I wasn't so sure that I wanted to go up to the house, but seeing Bull peeking through the blinds made me feel like I had to. With Hot Dog Guy tucked away in my pocket, I slowly got out of the car and made my way up the walk. The front yard was mostly dirt with a few patches of weeds, and there were more weeds growing through the cracks in the old concrete. Some of the boards on the front porch were broken, and when I climbed the steps I heard some kind of animal move beneath them. By the time I got to the front door I was really scared and ready to go back to the car, but I rang the doorbell anyway and waited. I didn't hear the doorbell so I rang it again, but still nothing happened. I was about to turn around when the door suddenly flew open and a smiling BullBorg was standing in front of me in full costume.

"The doorbell doesn't work," he said. "Do you want to come inside?"

"My daddy wants to talk to your parents first," I said, pointing towards the car. Daddy waved and I heard Parker laugh and say, "Look Daddy, another super hero!"

"My mother is at work," BullBorg said.

"What about your daddy?" I asked.

BullBorg looked down and his smile

disappeared. "I don't have a daddy."

I didn't even know what this meant because I thought everyone had a mommy and a daddy.

"What happened to your daddy?" I asked.

"I don't know. He left before I was born. I never even met him."

I looked back at Daddy. He asked what was going on, so I told BullBorg I would be right back and walked back to the car, where I told Daddy what BullBorg had told me.

"So he's home all alone?" Daddy asked. "Is there a babysitter inside?"

I walked back to the porch but didn't climb the steps. I asked BullBorg if there was a babysitter inside, but he shook his head.

"Ask him to come over here," Daddy said. I did so, but BullBorg shook his head again and remained in the doorway.

Daddy got out of the car and said, "Hi, Brian. Can you come over here for a minute? I just want to talk to you."

He shook his head again, and this time he shouted "No!"

"Brian, you're not in trouble," Daddy said. "I'm Morgan's father. I just want to talk to you. Morgan wants to play with you, but I need to make sure that there's an adult around."

Brian didn't respond. When Daddy closed the car door and took a step towards the house, Brian slammed the door shut and locked it.

Unsure of what to do next, I looked at Daddy. He didn't look like he knew what to do either, but finally he told me to come back to the car. I did so, but before I got back in I looked back at the house and saw the red cyborg eye peeking through the same window blinds as before.

I got back in the car, but Daddy remained standing and looking at the house.

"Okay, we're leaving now," Daddy announced towards the house loudly enough so that Brian would be able to hear him from inside. "You can come over to our house after school some time if you want, but I can't let Morgan play here without any adults around."

Daddy waited for a minute before getting back in the car. As we slowly pulled away, I watched the little red cyborg eye peeking through the blinds and felt worried that he was all alone in that beat up old house in this scary neighborhood and that it was going to be dark soon. Daddy looked at me in the rearview mirror and saw that I looked worried.

"He'll be okay, bud," he said. "I'm sure his mother will be home any minute."

I could tell Daddy was only saying that to make me feel better, so I tried not to think about it. But I couldn't stop thinking about it until I fell asleep that night.

CHAPTER 13

Over the weekend I was particularly annoyed at how much homework Mrs. Crabcake had assigned that was due on Monday morning. At this point I had given up hope that I would be able to transfer into Mr. Cooldude's class because every time I even mentioned his name, Mommy or Daddy would cut me off by saying, "You're not transferring into Mr. Cooldude's class".

During breaks in the marathon homework sessions I would go down to the playground hoping that Bull would be there, but he never was. I even figured out how to send Bull messages through my cyborg screen, but I never got a response. Finally on Sunday afternoon I asked Daddy if we could drive back to Bull's house to see if he was home and said that maybe this time his mother would be there since it was the weekend. But Daddy said that we couldn't go over there uninvited and reminded me that I would probably see Bull at school the next day.

Sure enough, Bull was back at his desk on Monday morning. But when I went over to say hello, he just looked at me and grunted. I was surprised by this considering how nice he had been to me at his house on Friday afternoon. Then I asked him if he wanted to come over after school and that my Daddy would help us with our homework and then we could play afterwards. In response he grunted even louder and ripped a piece of paper out of his notebook and crumpled it up into a ball. I thought he was going to throw it at me, but instead he put it into his mouth and started chewing it with loud, satisfied grunts like he was enjoying a good meal. I didn't stick around long enough to see if he actually swallowed it, but from my desk I did hear a gulp and a belch a few minutes later.

Recess was no better. Bull stood by himself leaning against the fence, and if anyone even looked in his direction, he grunted or snarled at them. At one point a stray kickball rolled to his feet and one of the third graders ran over to retrieve it. Before the kid had a chance to pick it up, though, Bull grabbed it and punted it a mile away. The kid was stunned by this and stood motionless until Bull growled at him so loudly that he ran away crying.

I had seen enough and started walking towards Bull. The closer I got, the louder he grunted. I stopped about five feet in front of him.

"Please stop grunting and scaring everyone," I said, but this only seemed to make him madder. He snarled loudly and his nostrils flared open like a real bull.

"Why are you so mad at me?" I asked. "And why are you being so mean to the other kids?"

"Because I'm Bull, and that's what Bull does."

"I thought you wanted to be a good guy," I said.

"I am a good guy," he said. "You're the bad guy."

"I'm not the bad guy!" I said. I couldn't believe what I was hearing.

"Yes you are," he said. "All of you are bad guys. Everyone in this stinking school and this stinking town and this stinking world is a bad guy. Now go away!"

He looked really scary, but my fear was being shoved aside by the anger burning inside me that was growing hotter by the second. I knew that if he made even a tiny little grunt I might not be able to control this anger, so I turned around and stormed away without looking back.

Fortunately recess was over and it was time for everyone to line up with their classes. I positioned myself at the front of our line knowing that Bull was probably going to go to the end of the line like he usually did. I was still very angry and didn't want to see him. While we were waiting to go back inside, I decided that when I got home I was going to do my homework as fast as I could and then go right down to the playground. I was going to make sure that he didn't show up and start scaring the kids away. As far as I was concerned, the Bull had declared himself an enemy to myself, my fellow schoolmates, the residents of West Plains, and all citizens of the free world.

CHAPTER 14

For the rest of the day I didn't turn around to look at Bull. When school was finally over I made sure to be first on the dismissal line so that I would be the first one out the door. When we got outside, Daddy and Parker were waiting for me in the pickup area as usual. Daddy asked if Brian was coming over, but I simply told him no and that I wanted to hurry home so I could finish my homework as fast as possible. Daddy could tell I was upset and that I didn't want to talk about it, so he didn't say anything. If whatever was bothering me meant that I would do my homework without complaining or hiding under the couch cushions or throwing toys across the room or talking back every time he said something, he would save the talk until I was done.

When we got home I tried to do my homework a little too fast and made a bunch of mistakes, which is what usually happens when I rush to get something done. Daddy says the trick to finishing homework quickly is to stay focused and take your time so that you will make less mistakes, which will save time later

because you won't have to sit there and correct all the ones you got wrong. *Blah blah blah.*

After I had finished, Daddy went over the mistakes on my math and reading questions and had me correct them. When I was finally done, I ran upstairs and quickly put on my HyperKid costume. I then ran back down the stairs and was ready to hurry to the playground but Daddy was waiting for me at the front door.

"Where are you going in such a hurry?" he asked.

"To the playground," I said.

"Did something happen at school today?"

"No."

"Then why do you seem to be upset and in such a hurry to run out the door? Tell me the truth, Morgan—did something happen with Brian at school today?"

Although I really didn't want to tell him, Mommy and Daddy have said a million times that a lie will make a bad situation worse, and that telling the truth will make the bad situation end sooner. So I told him the truth about what happened at recess.

"So, what are you planning to do now?" he asked.

"I'm going to make sure he doesn't show up and scare the kids away," I said.

"And how are you going to do that?"

I thought about it for a moment and realized that I wasn't really sure.

"Tell him to leave, I guess," I said.

"What if he doesn't leave?" Daddy asked.

"I can scare him away like I did the other day."

"How will you do that?"

"With my blasters, I guess."

"You know that you can only use your blasters in self-defense," Daddy said.

I was growing increasingly frustrated at the amount of questions Daddy was asking. I was tempted to use my hyper speed to run out the door, but I knew that doing so would mean that my days as HyperKid would probably come to an end.

"Listen, bud," Daddy said. "A wise man once said that with tremendous ability comes tremendous obligation. Or something like that. Now, I understand that you feel a sense of duty to protect the kids on the playground, and that's a good thing. And if Brian does show up and starts scaring them, you can certainly ask him to stop. If that doesn't work, you can even yell at him to stop. But unless he attacks you or the other kids, you can't try to physically force him to leave."

"What am I supposed to do if he doesn't listen?" I asked.

"Well, you can try to convince the other kids to leave if they haven't done so already. And then you can come home and tell me what happened. And then we can write up a complaint that we can submit to the principal or the school board—"

"I don't want to write!" I said, horrified at

the thought of doing any more writing than I already had to for school.

"Don't get caught up thinking about the writing part," Daddy said. "You can just talk about what happened and your cyborg system could probably transcribe it for you. I even have an app on my phone that can do that. But it might not even come to that. The point is, you can't just try to overpower him, and you can't break the rules to fix a problem. If you don't do things the right way, you might cause a bigger problem than the one you are trying to solve. If you're not careful, you might even get me and Mommy in trouble."

"But how can I get in trouble if he's the one doing bad things?" I asked. "He's the villain! Good guys are supposed to fight villains!"

"I don't think he sees himself as a villain," Daddy said. "He may not be so nice sometimes, but that doesn't mean he's a bad kid. Brian seems like a very troubled boy who has a very difficult life. Honestly, I feel terrible about what little we know about his situation. We are willing to help if we can, but we also have to be careful that his problems don't create problems for you—or for Mommy and I.

"We also have to be careful not to interfere. As much as we'd like to help him, we don't know the whole story and we can't just do something we think will help because that might actually cause more problems for him.

"Look at his situation—he said he never even met his daddy, and his mother might have to work a lot just to pay the rent and buy food. She might not get to spend as much time with Brian as she would like to, and he might have to spend a lot of time alone in that old house because she might not be able to afford a babysitter to keep him company and help him with his homework. That's rough. When kids don't get enough attention and don't have grown-ups around to teach them how to be responsible and how to behave properly, they often have more difficulty in school and make more mistakes than other kids.

"But making mistakes does *not* automatically make you a villain. Every person in the world makes mistakes, including adults like Mommy and I, your teachers, your friend's parents—everybody. It's frustrating to make mistakes, but you have to learn how to deal with them the right way and do what you can to correct them. Mistakes can also be very valuable because they teach you what *not* to do next time you are in a similar situation. The trick is to try not to get too frustrated and remember what you did wrong so that the next time you are in that same situation you will make a different choice…"

The *blah blah blah's* were approaching fast, but I was starting to understand what Daddy was saying and starting to feel less angry with Bull. It didn't seem fair that he might not have anyone around to help him and that he had to be in that scary old house all alone.

"But what should I do if he starts being mean again?" I asked when Daddy had finally stopped talking for a moment.

"If he's going to behave the way he did at school today, you're just going to have to try to stay away from him. It sounds like the other kids are already doing that, so you won't have to worry about protecting them so much. But his relationship with you is different than it is with the other kids. The two of you have this rare bond of being cyborgs that you are both adjusting to, and because of this he feels a connection with you—as a friend, as a rival, or both. He may also be confused how to react when someone is nice to him because he's not used to it. This may be why he acts so differently towards you at different times. I think he wants to be friends with you, but something might be making him afraid of accepting you as a real friend."

"Why would he be afraid?" I asked.

"Well, if he is afraid—and we don't know that—it probably has something to do with all that he's been through. He might be afraid of gaining a friend and then suddenly losing him, which is called a fear of abandonment. Or maybe he's just never had a real friend and he's frustrated because he doesn't know how to act with one. Whatever it is, these are pretty heavy issues, and they may or may not be why he behaves the way he does. But don't say anything to him about these things, and especially don't say anything to the other kids about what you know about Brian's parents or where he lives. The best thing you can do is just try to be nice to him, and if he's nice to you, great. If on another day he's not being nice, just stay away. But if on one of those days he's not being nice and you are trying to stay away from him but he still keeps bothering you, what do *you* think you should do?"

"Stay calm and ask him to please stop," I mumbled. Both Parker and I were very familiar with this question. Most of the time we get along fine and play nice together, but sometimes we get on each other's nerves—like when he starts taking my toys apart, or when he makes too much noise when I'm doing my homework, or when he distracts me when I'm playing video games. And sometimes I get on his nerves when I start acting a little too hyper.

"That's right," Daddy said. "And what should you do if you ask him politely to stop but he still keeps bothering you?"

"Stay calm and tell the teacher, or tell you," I mumbled.

"That's right. Otherwise, just try to be nice and maybe even say hello to him again tomorrow morning. If he grunts at you again, that's probably a good sign that you should stay away. Since you're still upset, you should probably stay away from him now and not go to the playground and see if you still feel the same way tomorrow. Bad decisions are often made when people are upset because they let their emotions take over their common sense. That's why *blah blah blah blah blah blah blah…*"

By the time Daddy had finished talking, I was exhausted. But I wasn't mad at Brian anymore. I decided that from now on whenever I felt mad at him, I should think about seeing him peeking through the blinds in that old house and how lonely he must be.

CHAPTER 15

Brian was already sitting at his desk when I got to school the next morning. He was staring down intently even though there were no notebooks or anything else in front of him to look at. He looked very sad, so I didn't approach him. Instead I said "Hi, Brian" and gave him a little wave, but he didn't respond.

Later that morning Mrs. Crabcake was reviewing some math problems on the board and was calling on us to answer questions about them. This always made me very nervous because my mind sometimes went blank when I was called on, even if it was an easy one that I definitely knew. After a few seconds of awkward silence I would finally just guess and get it wrong. It always made me feel stupid to get an easy problem wrong. Mommy and Daddy say that it's just anxiety, and that it has nothing to do with how smart I am. They say it's not unusual for smart people to feel anxious because sometimes they worry too much about getting the answer wrong instead of allowing their minds to focus on getting it right.

"When your mind gets distracted by worry, it has to work harder to get around the distraction to find the answer," Daddy once told me. "When your mind works harder, anxiety grows and grows until it takes over and shuts down the thought process. That's why it's helpful to try to stop the worry as soon as it starts by immediately locking in on the problem and blocking out everything else before it has a chance to get in. Nip it in the bud, bud. Hey, that's a good one. Do you see what I did there? I used the expression 'Nip it in the bud', and I also called you 'bud'. Get it? Morgan, are you with me? Hello?"

Blah blah blah. Mommy and Daddy should try sitting there with Mrs. Crabcake and all the other kids staring at you while your mind tries to add two mixed numbers.

Anyway, this morning Mrs. Crabcake called on Brian, but he didn't even look up. He had been staring down at his desk all morning. Even when Mrs. Crabcake kept calling his name louder and louder, he still didn't look up. Finally she walked back to his desk and tapped his shoulder, which made the other kids giggle. But what happened next shocked everyone in the classroom.

Brian suddenly started crying very loudly. Mrs. Crabcake asked him what was wrong, but he didn't answer. She asked him again more loudly, then she just started saying his name louder and louder until he finally responded.

"Nobody likes me!" he cried. "Nobody cares about me and I'm stupid and different

and I want to go home!"

He started crying even harder, and Mrs. Crabcake told him that he was going to have to go to the nurse's office until he calmed down.

I couldn't believe it. These were some of the very same things I usually said when I had major meltdowns. I knew exactly how he felt. Before I realized what I was doing, I got up and walked back to Brian's desk.

"I like you, Brian," I said. "And I know how you feel. Going to the nurse's office will help you feel better."

Brian started to calm down. Mrs. Crabcake asked if I would be willing to walk with him to the nurse's office, and I said yes. She then asked Brian if that would be okay, and he nodded.

Brian followed me to the front of the room. I had to focus on walking because I could feel every pair of eyes in that classroom watching our every move. It was a relief to finally get out into the hallway and hear the echo of Mrs. Crabcake's voice call the class back to attention behind us. Brian had managed to stop crying, but he was still sniffling.

"It will be okay," I said. "This happens to me all the time."

Although I felt bad for Brian, it made me

feel better knowing that I wasn't the only one who had meltdowns like this. Sometimes I feel really lonely during meltdowns because it seems like I'm the only one who has them and I start to wonder if something is wrong with me.

"Meltdowns are totally normal," Daddy once told me. "All kids have them, including the ones who act all cool and tough at school. You usually just don't see it with them because acting tough and cool in front of the other kids is very important to them, so they try really hard to hold it in until they get home.

"Even adults have meltdowns sometimes. That's because life is hard, and sometimes you feel overwhelmed. That's when they happen. Most people try to hide their meltdowns, although some don't—those people often wind up with their own reality TV shows. Others, especially kids, have a hard time controlling their emotions in public. That's kind of where you are right now, but it's not something to be overly concerned about. As you grow and become more mature and self-confident, you'll get better at controlling your emotions.

"Also keep in mind that there are plenty of other kids out there who have similar issues as you, including hyperactivity. It's really not that rare, so it shouldn't make you feel lonely.

There are millions of people in the world who are hyperactive. There may even be one or two others in your class, and a bunch more in your school. Sometimes you get so wrapped up in your own emotions that you don't notice the similarities you have with others. Similarities are not as noticeable as differences, so sometimes you don't see them right away.

"But even if you think you're the most unique person ever born and that nobody else understands you and that you're all alone in this great big world, every once in a while someone comes along who you realize is kind of like you and who does understand you and is able to appreciate you for who you truly are. Those are the people who have the potential of becoming true friends. It feels good when you encounter someone with whom you can be yourself and share your common experiences. While it's good to be different, it's also good to know that you're not alone."

Daddy was right. It did feel good knowing that there was someone else like me. Even though our lives were very different, Brian and I also had a lot of similarities. At that moment I knew exactly how he felt, and I think he knew that I knew. That was enough to help make us both feel better.

Neither of us said anything during our journey to the nurse's office, but it felt like there was a new understanding between us. When we arrived, Mrs. Stethoscope seemed surprised to see us and asked what was wrong.

"He's upset like I am sometimes," I said. "Maybe he could sit in my special chair because that usually helps me calm down."

"Thank you, Morgan," she said. "I'll take it from here. You can go back to class now."

I went back to class thinking that Brian was probably sitting in my special chair already starting to feel better. It felt good knowing that I was able to help someone without even having to be a super hero.

Back in the classroom, Mrs. Crabcake asked if everything was okay. I confidently told her that Brian would probably be just fine in a little while. She thanked me and then asked if I could tell her what eight times six was. Without even thinking about it or getting nervous, I said "forty eight". I was on a roll.

Brian came back to class just before lunch. Although he was no longer crying, he still looked sad. The other kids watched his every move as he made his way to his seat. His eyes were focused on the floor as he walked and he didn't look at anyone, including me.

The rest of the morning was uneventful. At lunch, though, the other kids at our class's table were whispering about Brian. They called him a crybaby and "Baby Bull", but he didn't give any hint that he could hear them even though I knew for sure that he could. He just kept eating his five roast beef sandwiches and the chunky red mystery sludge he brought in a plastic container every day. He didn't eat this sludge with a spoon but instead lifted the container to his mouth like he was finishing the last of the milk in a bowl of cereal.

Everyone stared at this ritual with fascinated horror, and someone would always say it looked like he was drinking blood, which, of course, made Gina scream. When he was finished, he would turn and grunt at us with the red stuff all over his mouth and then laugh when we showed our disgust. But today after finishing the sludge, he just calmly took a napkin out of his brown paper bag and wiped his mouth without looking in our direction.

Outside at recess, Brian was sitting on one of the swings and staring down at the dirt. The other kids sensed an opportunity for some revenge and started calling him "Baby Bull" from far away. When he didn't respond, they got closer and started saying it more loudly, but he continued to ignore them even when they were only a few feet away.

Then I noticed Robert pick up a small rock from the ground. Robert had been a regular victim of teasing over the years because of his habit of picking his nose and putting the boogers in his hair. The other kids said he had green hair because of all the boogers, but it wasn't really bright green but more like dirty blond with a green tint.

At first Robert just seemed to be inspecting the rock in his hand, but then he suddenly looked up at Brian and threw it towards him. Fortunately he missed, but I had seen enough.

"Stop it!" I yelled at Robert. Then I turned to the rest of the kids and shouted, "All of you, leave him alone!"

"You're a crybaby too!" Robert said.

"Oh, go pick your nose and eat it, Booger Boy!" I said. A message immediately appeared on my cyborg screen to "STAY CALM", but my insult worked because the kids turned their attention towards Robert and started calling him "Booger Boy". I felt bad about that, but this time he did kind of deserve it.

I went over and sat on the swing next to Brian.

"Go away," he mumbled without looking up at me.

"Don't listen to them," I said.

"Go away," he said more loudly.

"I'm just trying to help."

"Go away!" he shouted. I noticed the other kids turn and look towards us. I didn't understand why he was being mean to me when I was only trying to help, but then I thought about how I sometimes got annoyed when someone tried to help me at the wrong moment. I also remembered what Daddy said about not interfering, so I walked away and left him alone. The other kids left him alone too, but they didn't seem interested in playing with me either. So I spent the rest of recess walking around the playground by myself, but I couldn't help looking over towards Brian every few minutes.

When it was time to line up at the end of recess, Brian didn't get up from the swing. It wasn't long before the line was abuzz with kids anxious to see what he would do because none of us had ever seen a kid not come to lineup before. By the time we were heading inside, he still hadn't moved. One of the lunch aides, Mrs. Fripple, started walking towards him. Everyone wanted to see what would happen, but Mrs. Fripple was a really slow walker and we were inside before she got there.

Brian didn't come back to class for the rest

of the day. Just before it was time to go home, Mrs. Stethoscope poked her head in the door and asked Mrs. Crabcake if she could speak to her out in the hall for a moment. I tried turning up the volume on my super hearing, but the word "DISABLED" appeared on my cyborg screen. I figured they must be talking about Brian, and I began to wonder if something had happened. When Mrs. Crabcake came back in, she told us to listen very carefully.

"It has come to my attention," she started, but stopped cold to make individual eye contact with every one of us with the most frightening look ever. This was absolutely bone chilling coming from someone who looked scary even when she smiled.

"It has come to my attention," she started again, "that Brian was very upset about being picked on today at recess. He has had a very difficult time adjusting to his new home and his new school, so I am asking each and every one of you to say hello to him tomorrow morning and to do your best to make him feel welcome. And, if I hear about anyone teasing him or doing anything to purposely upset him, they will spend their recesses with me writing essays about the importance of being tolerant and respectful towards others, and their parents will be asked to come in and meet with the principal and I. Is that understood?"

Gina raised her hand.

"Yes, Gina," Mrs. Crabcake said.

"He's not nice to us," Gina said. "He's a mean bully. He grunts at us and chases us off the playground and then laughs at us."

"If anything like that happens again," Mrs. Crabcake said, "politely ask him to stop. If he doesn't stop, go tell one of the lunch aides, and also tell me what happened after recess. But do not start calling him names or bothering him back. Is that understood?"

"Yes, Mrs. Crabcake," the class mumbled.

The next morning, Mrs. Crabcake was waiting in the hall just outside the classroom. Brian was already seated at his desk inside. As

we went in, Mrs. Crabcake reminded each of us to say hello to Brian.

I followed Gina into the classroom. She said "hi" to Brian from about ten feet away and then stuck her tongue out at him. He didn't seem to notice. He still looked a little sad, but today it looked more like an angry kind of sad, not the crying kind of sad like yesterday. He didn't look up when I said hello, but I heard a slight grunt that almost sounded as if he was trying to say hello but couldn't get the word all the way out.

Brian was not out on the playground during recess. When we got back to class, he didn't come back until a few minutes later when he was brought by Mrs. Cheese, the school psychologist. I had spent much time with Mrs. Cheese since my kindergarten days, sitting in her office talking to her and drawing pictures and moving blocks around and that sort of stuff. This year Mommy and Daddy told me that I didn't have to see Mrs. Cheese anymore, but I kind of wish I did because she was really nice and it was good to get a break from trying to sit still while listening to the teacher in the boring old classroom. But I never had to go to her office during recess, which for me was the best part of the school day. As nice as she was, I would never ever ever never never EVER want to sit in her office instead of going to recess.

Then I thought about the kids picking on Brian during recess the day before. Maybe he would actually prefer to stay inside and talk to someone nice like Mrs. Cheese rather than be on the playground surrounded by kids who didn't like him. I guess that made sense. But if he was outside at recess the next day, I would make sure to try and play with him and be nice to him so that he would know that he had at least one friend and that he was not alone.

CHAPTER 16

At least ten times a day since the first day of school, Mrs. Crabcake would say something about the importance of a healthy diet and how we shouldn't eat junk food and stuff like that. This must be a pretty important subject for her because she kept a copy of a book titled *Beans: The Secret Ingredient to a Svelte Figure and a Healthy Body* on her desk. When we arrived in the morning and returned from recess in the afternoon, she was either eating or had just finished eating beans from little plastic containers, and the classroom would smell like a mixture of dirty socks and farts. The beans reminded me of the song Daddy always sings whenever we have beans at home:

Beans, beans, they're good for your heart
The more you eat, the more you fart

One day after recess, the smell in the room was particularly strong. When Gina walked in she very loudly said "Ewww, what's that smell?" and pretended to throw up. Mrs. Crabcake apologized for the smell and explained that she had just finished her bean salad and that the smell would go away in a few minutes.

What was worse (but much more hilarious) was that the beans always gave Mrs. Crabcake really bad gas and sometimes she would suddenly fart really loudly. Everyone would laugh whenever she ripped a loud one, but there was one day in particular when she was farting so much that it stopped being funny when we all started to feel like we were going to throw up for real.

After recess that day, Mrs. Crabcake was standing in front of her desk telling us about the first shot of the American Revolution being fired in Lexington when she suddenly stopped talking mid-sentence and became as still as a statue. She remained motionless for several moments until there was a loud pop and a flash as if a firecracker had gone off behind her. All of us shuddered in our seats and let out a startled gasp, and, of course, Gina screamed. At first I thought Mrs. Crabcake had set up some kind of special effect that was supposed to mimic one of the muskets that the Patriots used, which I thought was pretty cool despite the timing being a little off. But I quickly realized that this was not the case when Mrs. Crabcake's face turned bright red and she apologized for the "excessive gas emissions", explaining that her stomach was not agreeing with her and that she was beginning to suspect that the beans had something to do with it.

She tried to resume her lesson, but she kept squirming and reaching behind her as if her bottom was bothering her. Then I noticed some smoke behind her, and on her desk a couple of small flames had appeared on the stack of math tests we had taken that morning. At that moment I realized that her explosive last fart had caused the back side of her dress and the stack of tests to catch fire. Considering how poorly I knew I had done on the test, the thought crossed my mind to let them burn before saying something. But I knew right away that this would be a bad decision and immediately raised my hand.

Just as Mrs. Crabcake was about to call on me, she froze again. Another explosive flash shot out of her bottom followed by a long, loud fart. The gas from the fart hit the flames on her desk and created a stream of fire that made it look like a flamethrower was being shot out of her butt. The fire stream reached all the way to the bulletin board on the front wall and ignited the papers and posters. Moments later the front of the classroom was engulfed in flames.

The fire alarms went off and the sprinklers started spraying water from the ceiling, but a moment later they stopped. Now all the kids were screaming, including me, until a bright red message flashed on my cyborg screen that said "SPRINKLER SYSTEM MALFUNCTION: DEPLOY FIRE ARMOR". Suddenly I was being covered with shiny gold metal armor similar to Recycled Metal Man's "Build 451". The same thing was happening to Brian, only his armor was bright red. My HyperKid logo was on my chestplate, and a new professional looking version of the BullBorg logo was on Brian's. We both had larger versions of our cyborg arms, and our other arms now had huge detachable blasters connected to them. BullBorg's helmet had a dark tinted window covering his entire face and bullhorns on the crown. On his face window I saw the reflection of my own helmet, which had a tinted visor and my HyperKid "H" logo on the crown.

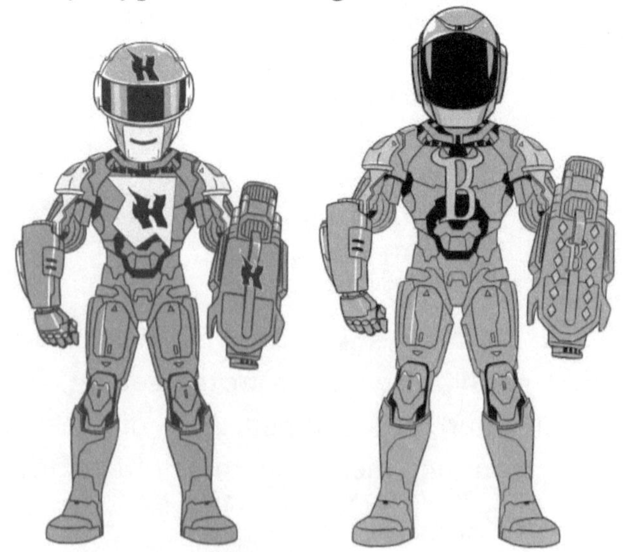

A message flashed on my screen that said "DEPLOY FIRE EXTINGUISHER". I detached my blaster and pointed it at Mrs. Crabcake's butt. Then another message appeared that said "TARGET LOCKED", and the blaster started shooting fire extinguishing foam that quickly doused the flames on the back of her dress.

Meanwhile, BullBorg was using his blaster to put out the flames blocking the doorway. When those were out, he started directing the other kids out of the classroom and kept saying with an electronic voice, "Please remain calm and exit in an organized manor per normal fire drill procedures. No pushing or shoving, please. Thank you and have a nice day."

After the other kids had all exited, BullBorg joined me in dousing out the rest of the flames in the room. Mrs. Crabcake was frantically telling us to leave, but we continued to work until the fire was completely out. When we were finally heading towards the door, our armor quickly retracted and we were back in our civilian clothes by the time we reached the hallway. Mrs. Crabcake followed us as we caught up to our class line among the rest of the classes being evacuated to the playground just as we normally did during regular fire drills.

When we got outside, no one said anything to Brian and I at first. Everyone was distracted watching the fire trucks and an ambulance arrive. Several firefighters jumped off the truck and ran into the building, but a few minutes later two of them came back out holding their helmets and masks. They looked confused and kept shrugging their shoulders as they explained to the captain that the fire had already been put out.

After the excitement of the arriving firefighters had died down, the other kids finally started turning around to look at Brian and I at the end of the line. Gina, who was never shy about anything, left her spot in line and came right up to us.

"What the heck was that?" she asked. "Are you guys super heroes or something?"

"No," I said. "We're just regular normal kids, except we can do some extra stuff too. That's all."

"And all of you cry sometimes too," Brian said. The statement seemed a bit off-topic at the moment, but Gina seemed to know where he was coming from.

"I know," she said calmly. "I'm sorry about calling you names, especially since you guys are super heroes and all." She then remained quiet for a moment before her face suddenly lit up and she said very loudly, "OMG, that was *SOOOOOO* totally awesome!" She had said it so loudly that a couple of the firefighters looked in our direction.

"I liked the part when you guys put on that armor like Recycled Metal Man," Robert said. "That was the coolest thing I've ever seen in real life! Can you do that again?"

Robert's request got the rest of the kids in our class excitedly asking us to put the armor back on. It occurred to me that I had no idea how I did it the first time and had no idea how to do it again. Mrs. Crabcake was over at the ambulance being looked at, so there wasn't a teacher watching our class. The excitement on our line was starting to attract the attention of kids from other classes, but Brian was able to quiet our classmates down by raising his hands like he had something important to say.

"Please remain calm," he said. "My name is Brian, and this here is my friend Morgan." He looked at me and put a hand on my shoulder. "Like he said, we're just normal kids. But if anyone is in trouble and needs some help, I'm sure we can convince those super hero guys to come back. They're *both* good guys, you know."

CHAPTER 17

From then on the other kids were nice to Brian and I, and they were always asking when BullBorg and HyperKid were going to come back. We told them that they could sometimes be found at the playground after school, but lately things had been calm and they liked to keep a low profile. That's not saying that Brian and I hadn't tried to make the special armor appear again, but every time we told our cyborg systems to deploy the fire armor we got an error message about restricted access.

Meanwhile, Mommy had also managed to get in touch with Brian's mother, which was difficult because she had three jobs and was hardly ever home. Mommy is the kind of lawyer who helps families in need of legal assistance, so she was able to set Brian up with a social worker and an affordable babysitter for when his mother was at work. Brian's mother also gave permission to let him come over after school a couple of days a week, and Daddy said he would help both of us with our homework on those days.

Brian and I also formed an official alliance called "The West Plains Super Hero League". Mommy agreed to make a new BullBorg costume for Brian to replace the one he had made himself, and Daddy helped us set up the alliance website, which we would use to make official announcements and sell BullBorg and HyperKid t-shirts and other merchandise to supplement our meager allowances. Brian actually didn't even know what an allowance was and nearly fainted when I told him that my parents gave me money every week for cleaning my room and sweeper-mopping the upstairs floors.

When BullBorg's new costume was ready, we announced that the West Plains Super Hero League would be making an appearance at the playground on Friday afternoon after school. Fridays were one of the days Brian came over, so when we got to the house we changed into our costumes and headed right back out.

At the playground we were shocked to find a huge crowd of kids, teachers, and a fire truck parked with the firefighters lined up next to it. Brian's mother was also there, and Mommy, Daddy, and Parker had secretly followed us from the house. The crowd started cheering and clapping when we arrived, and Mrs. Crabcake stepped towards us and said, "Here are the two heroes!"

Mrs. Crabcake led us to the fire truck, where we were greeted by the mayor of West Plains, Maria Martinez. She introduced herself and shook our hands, then thanked us for our service. One of the firefighters then handed her a bullhorn, but just before she was about to speak, Mrs. Crabcake interrupted her by asking if she could say something first. Mayor Martinez nodded and handed her the bullhorn.

"First of all," Mrs. Crabcake said, "I would like to announce that I have officially ended my bean diet, and I strongly advise everyone not to buy the book *Beans: The Secret Ingredient to a Svelte Figure and a Healthy Body*." The crowd cheered. "More importantly," she continued, "I want to personally thank these two brave young heroes—what are your names again?"

"I *am* BullBorg," Brian said.

"I *am* HyperKid," I said.

"Thank you, BullBorg and HyperKid, for your bravery," Mrs. Crabcake said. "Because of your swift actions, not one person was injured, except for a few minor burns on my derriere!"

The crowd cheered again. Mrs. Crabcake wanted to say more, but Mayor Martinez thanked her and took back the bullhorn.

"On behalf of the City of West Plains," Mayor Martinez said, "I would also like to personally thank BullBorg and HyperKid for their heroic actions. Thanks to them, nobody was hurt, and the damage from the fire was limited to the classroom, which saved the taxpayers of this city a heck of a lot of money!"

The crowd cheered again. Mayor Martinez then made a hand signal to one of her security guards, who was holding two giant old-fashioned metal keys. The guard handed her one of the keys, which was so big and heavy that she had to hold it with two hands.

"On behalf of the City of West Plains," she said, "I am pleased to present BullBorg and HyperKid each with a key to the city!"

The crowd went wild. A photographer came over and asked us to pose for a picture that would be in the newspaper. BullBorg and I struck our best super hero poses while Mayor Martinez held one of the giant keys.

After the picture was taken, BullBorg asked Mayor Martinez what the key opened. She laughed and said it was the key to the hearts of the citizens of West Plains. We were both disappointed with this answer. I was kind of hoping it would open a giant castle door, or maybe a huge high-tech hover carrier that would be our new headquarters.

Suddenly there was a huge "BOOM" and explosion in the sky above the baseball field. At first I thought that it might be part of a fireworks show that they had planned for us, but then a black spot appeared in the sky at the point of explosion. The spot started growing larger and larger until it became a tunnel streaked with blue lightning. I used my super cyborg vision to zoom in on the tunnel, and at the other end of it I saw a night sky dotted with millions and millions of stars. At that moment I realized that this was not some fireworks show or unusual weather event but a wormhole just like the ones villains from other galaxies often use to travel to Earth.

I was about tell BullBorg what I thought it was when some sort of object moving inside the wormhole blocked out the stars. The object grew larger and began to take shape as it approached the opening on our end, but it wasn't until it was completely out of the wormhole that I recognized it to be an ARC (alien robot cyborg). A surge of panic shot through my human parts while my cyborg sensors started working at hyperspeed. A few seconds later a "CODE RED" warning message appeared on my cyborg screen:

```
NAME: ALIEN-BOT
SPECIES: ALIEN ROBOT CYBORG - A.K.A. "ARC"
ORIGIN: GALAXY Y-90125
CYBORG METEOR TYPE: FORTIFIED GALACTITE
CLASSIFICATION: VILLAIN - EXTENSIVE CRIMINAL RECORD,
   WANTED IN 23 GALAXIES
***USE EXTREME CAUTION***
...CONTACTING SVEN'S GARAGE FOR EQUIPMENT UPGRADES...
```

The crowd began to murmur nervously. Alien-Bot hovered over second base and started turning its head slowly as if performing a scan. It had arms and legs like a regular humanoid, but it also had four long tentacles emerging from its back. Its body was a metal skeleton with a complex system of wires and other parts inside of it. Its hands and tentacles had pointed razors for fingers, and its feet had shorter razors for toes. Its head looked like a metal brain with a face on the front of it. Its teeth were shiny triangular razors. And, against the backdrop of the otherwise peaceful cloud-puffed blue sky, its red cyborg eye glowed ominously as it scanned the crowd before stopping and locking on BullBorg and I. The eye looked exactly like the ones we had.

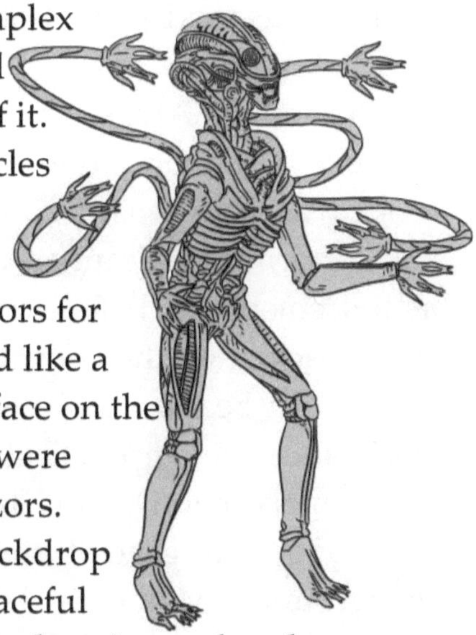

While Alien-Bot was as scary looking as any ARC I had ever seen in a comic book or a movie, what really frightened me was the thought that it was probably there because of BullBorg and I—but not to celebrate us as heroes. I looked at BullBorg and he looked back at me, and I was pretty sure he was thinking the same thing, that this was our call to the big leagues. We would now move from the playground to the intergalactic battlefield of good versus evil. The unlit side was now aware of us, and Alien-Bot had probably been sent to find us.

Although ARCs are not known to be capable of human emotions, Alien-Bot almost looked as if it was giving BullBorg and I a sinister grin as it scanned us. And, as unlikely as it seemed, just before it turned and warped itself back into the wormhole, I could have sworn I heard an electronic voice say "resistance is impractical" followed by an electronic version of the bully laugh that not long ago had echoed throughout this very playground. Moments later the wormhole closed and the sky was once again all blue with puffy white clouds as if nothing had happened.

"We're in trouble," I said to BullBorg.

BullBorg shrugged. "I'm not worried," he said.

At first I was shocked to hear him say this. But later when I mentioned it to Mommy and Daddy, they said that an alien robot cyborg may not seem scary to Brian compared to all the stuff he had already been through in his life. I understood what they meant, but I was still scared. And it didn't help to think about what Mayor Martinez had said to BullBorg and I just after Alien-Bot was gone.

"The city needs you two," she said with that *we're-counting-on-you-to-save-us* look that mayors and commissioners and presidents usually give super heroes when villains show up. "I want you guys to work for me. But make sure your homework gets done first before you show up for work."

Later that night I had trouble falling asleep. I called Daddy up to my room because it usually helps me fall asleep if he or Mommy counts to twenty for me. But tonight that didn't even help. My mind just wouldn't slow down.

"What's wrong, bud?" he asked.

"I don't know if I want to work for Mayor Martinez," I said. "This is getting too serious. I'm scared."

"You don't have to decide now. And whatever you decide is okay with Mommy and I. We're already very proud of you and will support whatever you decide. But why don't you take a vacation from being a super hero for a while. The decision will eventually come to you on its own."

My mind began to relax and soon I was asleep. I dreamed that Alien-Bot came back to the playground and tried to take everyone's toys, but BullBorg and I were able to easily defeat him. There was another celebration, and this time Mayor Martinez did give us keys to a hover carrier that was so big it could be seen from West Plains *and* East Plains. She also gave us keys to castles for our families to live in, but in the dream Mommy said she didn't want to move out of our house but that maybe the castle could be our vacation home.

When I woke up the next morning, the decision was already made in my mind. I knew what I was going to do, but it was Saturday, and at the moment I just wanted to eat my breakfast while watching my favorite TV show, *The Super Hero Super Half-Hour*, and then play video games. I didn't want to think about being a super hero. I just wanted to be the normal nine year old kid who can be a bit hyperactive at times but is otherwise no more unusual than any other kid. And all those other kids who seem smarter and more popular and are able to sit still and pay attention—they all have their own problems to deal with, and many of them are a lot worse than mine. I'm pretty lucky to be who I am.

THE END

ABOUT THE AUTHORS

Emerson Daub is a fourth grade student who loves to play with toys and has a healthy interest in cyborgs and super heroes. Having already written a children's book with his father Richard about their pet cats titled *Spaulding and Zoom,* Emerson expressed interest in writing a new book that combined two of his favorite interests. In writing this new book, Emerson, who has a very creative mind and active imagination, sat down with his father and in one sitting made up the story that would become *The Adventures of HyperKid: HyperKid v BullBorg*. Richard, who at one time had been a reporter but admittedly has very limited knowledge of cyborgs and modern super heroes, took extremely diligent notes and asked many detailed questions about the characters and the story. After this marathon session, Richard typed up the notes and gave them a voice. Over the following months, the father and son duo worked together to refine the prose into a tight but entertaining first person narrative. They hope the finished work will be enjoyed by all who read it and that it will serve as inspiration for everyone to rise above their personal obstacles and not let them hinder the pursuit of their goals and dreams.

Alien-Bot wants to save his home planet of Alania and make it great again—and he is willing to destroy the entire universe to do it. Can HyperKid and BullBorg stop him? Find out in this incredible sequel, where Morgan and Brian learn why they were chosen to become cyborgs, and meet the *other* cyborg super hero from Earth who battles Alien-Bot with them at the very end of the universe.

www.ingramcontent.com/pod-product-compliance
Lightning Source LLC
Chambersburg PA
CBHW050451110726
47899CB00003B/895